History Keeps Me
Awake at Night

History Keeps Me Awake at Night

Christy Edwall

GRANTA

Granta Publications, 12 Addison Avenue, London, W11 4QR

First published in Great Britain by Granta Books, 2023

Text and illustrations copyright © Christy Edwall, 2023

A CIP catalogue record for this book
is available from the British Library.

1   3   5   7   9   10   8   6   4   2

ISBN 978 1 78378 842 2
eISBN 978 1 78378 843 9

Typeset in Garamond by Patty Rennie
Printed and bound by CPI Group (UK) Ltd, Croydon, CR0 4YY

www.granta.com

For Gerard Whyte,
Musketeer

Private lives are not historical.

OCTAVIO PAZ

I think nothing ever disappears, said the Mexican. There are people, and animals, too, and even objects, that for one reason or another sometimes seem to want to disappear, to vanish. Whether you believe it or not, Harry, sometimes a stone wants to vanish, I've seen it. But God won't let it happen. He won't let it happen because He can't. Do you believe in God, Harry? Yes, Señor Demetrio, said Harry Magaña. Well, then, trust in God, He won't let anything disappear.

ROBERTO BOLAÑO, 2666

1

Strange as it might seem, I never dreamed about them, the missing forty-three. They were as hidden from my unconscious as they were hidden from the world when I was awake. It's too easy to expect revelations from sleep, and they were nothing if not difficult, even if, of course, the difficulties they posed were no fault of their own. It had something to do with the lawlessness of the country in which they were born; with the pull of those names I never looked up on a map – Sinaloa, the glide of a sand snake, the bend in the river; Oaxaca, the tang of beef hacked from a hanging carcass. Even before I came across them, I liked to read stories set in dusty cafés or cantinas, on the streets, or on the stairs of cathedrals, under gruesome sunsets, or beneath the hot roof of noon. I could say *por favor* and *gracias*. I used the words on a holiday to Barcelona when the waiters made me ask for a coffee in mangled Spanish, a play they put on for each other as they stood along the bar of an empty café, polishing glasses in an officious show of dedication. *Si, si, claro*, the waiters (always men, in Barcelona) would say, vying to make my coffee but never spilling a drop on their white shirts or on the spotless towels they wore at their waists.

And maybe there was a pull to this lawlessness, or maybe it was because there are certain crimes that capture the imagination – the assassination of presidents, the kidnapping of children, perverse crimes of passion which end with dismemberment or decapitation – that I remember exactly where I was when I first read about the forty-three missing students three years ago: Starbucks, Goodge Street, the last day of September.

I had finished an interview for an internship at *Figura* and it had gone unpredictably well. During the interview, the managing editor, Marcello Greave, sitting cross-legged in a worn Chesterfield and drinking espresso that had come from a machine awkwardly hulked in the hallway, asked me what I thought about Bruce Nauman, Maria Abramovich, Io Frajmund. I said I'd never heard of Io Frajmund and that was it, I was in. This was no great credit to me – with a name like Io Frajmund, anyone could tell it had been invented – but the look on Greave's face suggested the novelty of admitting ignorance. He offered me an espresso and I accepted. He took no steps towards making the espresso appear, which I assumed was part of the interview, a test either of my patience or of my initiative. I was either supposed to pretend that the espresso had never been offered, or to gently suggest that it must have been lost on the way to his office: a busy editorial assistant, cup in hand, must have paused to answer the phone and been caught by the printers demanding the fulfilment of their latest invoice. I was so undecided between the two positions that I heard nothing of Greave's conversation until he suddenly stood, a leggy man in woollen trousers and chestnut monk straps, laying his teacup on top of the ragged pile of magazines and newspaper supplements heaped on a nearby footstool, and standing on the seat of the rusty Chesterfield to reach the top row of the white built-in floor-to-ceiling bookshelves.

'You might as well get to know our house style,' he said, tossing back issues down to me. 'Don't judge us by the type-face. Both of those are from Duncan's day. We had a real come-to-Jesus moment, so to speak, after he left. I could tell you horrors about the books – but perhaps we should spare that until you've been with us at least a week. Something to look forward to, yes?'

The name Duncan meant nothing to me, but I sat pleasantly under the weight of the back issues piled on my lap. They were printed on heavy paper interleaved with glossy advertisements, and priced at £5.95 (Winter 2001) and £6.95 (Spring 2003) respectively. The current value (Autumn 2014) was set at £14. Greave suggested my duties might include tedious tasks such as answering the phones and occasional correspondence, and being asked to do the odd café run, but they tried to give interns a chance to prove themselves, he said: a line-edit here and there, covering a gallery opening for the smaller listings, brief interviews, etc, etc. Money was not to be expected, he said without embarrassment, but there would be perks: artists dropping by, gallerists on the phone, free books, the chance of my name in print.

'Fuck, the espresso,' he said, as we stood and shook hands over the coffee table. 'It slipped my mind.' As he ushered me out of his room I saw tartan bed slippers under his desk and a sickly plant at the window, its pot full of ashes. 'When you next come in we'll give you a tutorial on the machine. You'll have an endless fountain of real Italian espresso in no time at all.'

I did not grasp then what Marcello Greave meant: that hardly anyone else in the office knew how to use the espresso machine, with the exception of Imogen, Marcello's assistant, who hated it and was determined to slough off espresso duty at the first opportunity, and that it would become my sole responsibility to conjure drams of coffee whenever a staff member shouted for it. This distinction extended to an office-wide attribution to myself of unmerited expertise in the machine only moments after I had been taught its basic mechanisms. Whenever the espresso machine went on the blink, the editorial team would stand apprehensively around me, waiting to see what feat of engineering I might pull off. I did not know that, from my first day, Greave would refer to the painter William Kentridge as my 'compatriot', since we had the accident of South African citizenship in common. Nor did I know anything about Thomas J. Farber – the American venture capitalist whose middle name, we thought, must stand for Jefferson – who had bought the magazine for his second wife, Deirdre. It was Deirdre, or Didi as she liked to be called, whose minor fantasies the editorial staff had been acquired to entertain: invitations to private parties, samples from ingratiating advertisers, small doses of uppers and downers which Didi wheedled from each of them at one time or another, and an endurance for her boundless and almost legendary capacity to reconfigure the truth, including the painful hour when they did not or could not contradict Didi's insistence that Mark Rothko was still alive and at work on a new commission for a private collector whose name she was not at liberty to disclose. I knew nothing at that point about the tempers that broke down so spectacularly between all the inhabitants of the office in the basement of the Farbers' house on Bedford Square before the printing of the newest issue, or about the delirious relief that followed a successful launch. I did not know that Farber had chosen Bedford Square because, as a hypochondriac, he liked how near it was to the London School of Hygiene & Tropical Medicine; or that the junior members of the editorial team were constantly mutinously plotting the transfer of the magazine to the hipper fringes of Clapham or Hoxton; or that, on principle, we never mixed with the pricks at the Paul Mellon Centre or Sotheby's Institute.

Knowing none of this on that September day, I walked towards Gower Street with the weight of the back issues in my arms, a motor roaring in my heart. I walked blindly, dangerously, across the streets, admiring the sound of my shoes and the neatness of the square, the peppered Georgian brick, the plaster arches and black doors, the gauze curtains draped in every window. I'll go there on my breaks, I thought, passing the locked garden in the centre of Bedford Square with its dense, secluded paths, its borders of plane and holly. In summer I'd turn brown from hours of eating avocado wraps and reading *Bonjour Tristesse* on one of the benches.

When I'd applied to City University the year before, Nina, my mother, who as an English teacher was by no means a pragmatist, thought it a stupid idea to try a master's in journalism. She reminded me of the staff layoffs, the insecure contracts, the shrinking revenues, the large takeovers, the insurgency of digital media, the amateurization of the news in an era of citizen reportage – but I was sold on it. I saw myself taking notes, interviewing bystanders, taking a taxi late at night when the phone rang. I applied for the internship at *Figura* because I had insisted on arts reporting, and my placement at the *Telegraph* arts desk had not yielded a job offer – they hired no one, my minder confessed to me, and if they did, it was solely to manage the digital listings. Their writing came from stringers largely, or from the kind of people who could buy art as well as write about it. But I hadn't really wanted to write about art – at least, I hadn't wanted to write reviews no one read. What I really wanted, which I had never told anyone, was to detect forgeries; or rather, since I was never going to be the one to uncover a fake, I'd be the ear the conservator or art historian, with her PhD, her position at an institute or museum, her small lunches in the Luxembourg Gardens, whispered into; I'd hand her the shovel.

I'd read somewhere that the National Art Museum of China in Beijing, concerned for the safety and condition of the priceless artefacts in its galleries, had commissioned thousands of fakes, and that the paintings on the walls, the sculptures and the vases people lined up to see and for which they'd paid the price of admission were mere copies of the originals stored in the basement. In London, the discovery of an artwork's forgery led to its devaluation, to the damaged reputation of the museum or gallery which had wrongly authenticated it, and to the anger of the humiliated public who had been taken in. At the National Art Museum of China, however, the public were unconcerned. This, I thought, was an article in itself – this was well worth a newspaper picking up the tab for a flight to Beijing. But *Figura*, a quarterly, was uninterested in revelations. And although I'd been told that you can rub shoulders with anyone in London, I'd never met anyone with the least desire to send me to China.

The gig at *Figura* wasn't my first job in the art world. The year before I enrolled in the journalism course at City, and from time to time afterwards, I worked as a gallery assistant at Tate Modern. The phrase 'gallery assistant' had seemed to promise exclusive drinks receptions; tense hangings with temperamental curators; errands run for grateful artists who would admit, in private, their uncertainties; and eventually, if I was lucky, invitations to write for the catalogue or contribute instructive captions to whichever Hirst or Riley or Martin the museum had excavated from its storerooms. The primary expectation made of me, however, was that I would arrive for my shift in black like a jobbing musician. The second was that I would be able to use the iPad with which I was entrusted. Visitors, I was warned, would come up to me and ask improbable questions. They would demand to know where the Chris Ofili painting they'd seen ten years before was hung; they would want to know how to find a Blake that was held at the other Tate, Tate Britain. They might want to know, I was told, what had happened to the sunflower seeds from the Ai Weiwei installation once it had been dismantled.

But even this proved to be intellectually optimistic: I was mostly asked directions to the toilet. Visitors had devices of their own if they wanted to check the relationship between Gerhard Richter and the Second World War, or to review the provenance of a late Bonnard. It was only after meeting my fellow gallery assistants that I learned how low the bar for hiring was: well over half of them had no qualification in art. One of them, Emma, said her favourite painter was William Holman Hunt. Another, Priscilla, had become a gallery assistant to prove to her father that she could hold a job, even though she was planning her wedding to a consultant in Hong Kong. I had a middling degree from University College London, where my fellow art history students and I spent our leisure time dividing works into Art and Not Art, a conversation which launched us into vicious rows in student pubs, where eventually one or another of us would become seriously offended, tipping glasses or knocking over chairs as we stalked out. This was a conversation I tried to repeat with the only real artist among the gallery assistants, a woman in her forties called Patty Bercow, who was recently divorced and working at the Tate while she took art classes in the evening. I'd never tried to paint: I prided myself on knowing my limitations. In the course of being around art people at university, or at third- and fourth-tier gallery openings, you met friends of friends who called themselves artists because they made video diaries and took hours to choose their clothes. There was another class of people who called themselves writers – or worse, poets – because they sat in cafés with Moleskine notebooks or laptops, cut their own fringes, smoked beautifully, and racked up what they called Experience. But it was really all just scraps of language: nothing more than a knack for a phrase.

At the museum, we worked from ten to six in half-hour rotations, dreaming of a shift in a corner seat. Every now and then a curatorial team would come by, the men balding in unison; the women, thin and breastless, wearing polo necks in winter and linen in summer. There was something god-like about them, these multilingual men and women who had lovers in Milan and Berlin, catalogue drafts on their desks, and invitations to gallery openings in their inboxes.

Those old hierarchies were behind me, I thought on that late-September day after the *Figura* interview. Here comes the fifth column! I was walking against the Gower Street current, passing under the Babylonian eye of Senate House, past the muttering parade of second-class hotels, past travellers whose wheeled suitcases raked up complaints, and others drawn south-east by the imperial witchcraft of the British Museum. They came from all over the world, breaking away from their beginnings, fragments looking for other dislocated things, the way widowers find wounded crows.

As I walked north, the hoarded shards of the past grew dim, loosened their hold, becoming nothing more than plaster, coin, rock. That day I could have cheerfully tossed them in the gutter. I was radiating a happiness so undiluted that I was sure the passers-by could feel it wrinkling the air around them, a chemical cocktail of joy pure enough to make my blood fizz. When I walked past the tube station at Goodge Street and into Starbucks, I opened the door like Hemingway entering the Ritz after the Armistice, demanding every bottle of champagne in the cellar. Too jangled and skittery after my triumph to sit quietly and wait for my coffee, I hovered near the counter, close enough to feel the jets of hot steam in the pipes of the espresso machine whistling through my ears. Someone had left a limp copy of the *Guardian* near a pile of torn sugar packets and damp paper napkins, and I leafed through it. I passed over the portraits of protesters in Hong Kong and articles on the chancellor's tax credit cuts, vaguely looking for the editorial on the Turner prize. When my name was called and I'd collected my coffee, I came back to find the newspaper open at a page with a headline that read: 'Students still missing after deadly attack by Mexican police and gunmen'. Below, a photograph from Reuters showed five girls sheltering beneath a black tarp. It was night, and the girls held long white candles, the kind you'd set in the neck of an old wine bottle. Their mood was uncertain. They waited with a watchfulness that might let out a strained giggle. Below the headline, I read:

IGUALA, Mexico—. Buried in a landscape often referred to as Tierra Caliente (the Hot Lands), the city of Iguala sits at the crossroads of criminal activity in the state of Guerrero. The local cartel, Guerreros Unidos, a splinter from the Beltrán Leyva cartel which split into factions in 2010, is rumoured to control the city. Both Guerreros Unidos and members of the municipal police—who are known to be in the cartel's pay—are believed to be responsible for the disappearance of over forty students following a series of attacks carried out on the night of September 26th, whose whereabouts are still unknown. An initial total of 57 individuals were believed to have disappeared after masked gunmen opened fire on a convoy of buses in which the students were travelling on Friday night. Fourteen have since been located through reports from relatives, hospital staff, or locals who offered shelter. The reason behind the attacks is still unknown.

There's a kind of recognition that comes from meeting in life what you know from books, a form of déjà vu which deserves its own name: a technical term like the ones we learned from Mrs Lurie when we were sixteen and were taught to recognize the pathetic fallacy, which we only partially understood. That September I had been re-reading Bolaño, a writer I had first discovered on the shelves of a rented flat on that long-ago holiday to Barcelona, and whom I would always associate with dust, sweat and old drunk men looking at my chest while they told me to watch out for thieves. In fact, I had taken Bolaño's *2666* with me to the interview that day: it was in my handbag, taking up the handbag's body like the inner tray of a matchbox fits into its sleeve, a talisman as much as a guarantee against boredom.

And so while on any other day I would have turned the page of the newspaper as carelessly as a channel surfer finds one programme no more interesting than the previous one, or in the way that you find yourself clicking through a column of recommended videos on YouTube, not even waiting for the first clip to finish before you begin a second, and then a third, that day I felt a jolt, an electric charge, the jagged shimmer that comes before an ocular migraine. It's real, it said, Bolaño's novel had been transcribed into life. There never was a separation.

'Two students were killed as a result of the attacks of September 26,' I read on, 'and one left in a coma. A third student was later discovered in an allegedly mutilated state, one of his eyes gouged out and the skin flayed from his face.'

I found a table by the window, pushed the copies of *Figura* I had been carrying to the side of the table, and continued to read. The violent events in Iguala, the article said, were the tip of the iceberg: a politician assassinated in an Acapulco restaurant, five murdered around the corner in a poor barrio, and now students of a radical teachers' college having disappeared without a trace. It seemed that the state prosecutor, Iñaki Blanco, was planning to issue a charge of 'forced disappearance'.

Under the influence of the coffee and the residual adrenaline from the interview, and from the echo, stronger now and growing stronger still, of Bolaño's novel (wasn't it, after all, a hunt for that sinister and ghostly novelist Archimboldi, an extended investigation into his disappearance, as well as into the deaths of the hundreds of women discovered in the deserts of Sonora?), I could feel myself thinking in new peaks, making new glittering leaps of association. I'd always thought of disappearance as involuntary, or as involuntary as the loss of something exposed to a greater force: the outer wall of a ruined fort collapsed into the sea, a path grown over with brambles and hedge, an important paper – a receipt, a summons – slipped unseen down the back of a desk. The phrase that appeared in the article, 'forced disappearance', was a contradiction in terms, because whoever *did* the forced disappearing could not make the object disappear for themselves. They watched it fade, and couldn't help mark the place. They could never be amazed by the vanishing act; they would never unsee the strings, trapdoors and decoys. The students were a disappearing ink for which only the enforcers, whoever they were, held the reagent.

But I knew this spark, this alertness. It was the pulse I had felt when I was thirteen and in my Lord Lucan phase. That is what I mean by certain crimes capturing the imagination. For several years I had cut articles out of newspapers and glued them one after another into a hardbound A4 school notebook: sightings of the murderous earl in Argentina and Angola and Perth, rumours of his travels through Goa, confirmations of his death in Switzerland. If Nina, my mother, wasn't the instigator – if she hadn't actually directed my attention to the picture of the man with the oiled hair and luxuriant moustache; if she hadn't said, as I seem to recall she did, that my father had resembled Lord Lucan, only his hair was not so thick – then she certainly encouraged my interest, taping interviews as they appeared late at night, enlisting her sister in Wales to send clippings from the *Mail* and the *Sun*.

Neither my high spirits nor the article which fed them seemed to have anything to do with the photograph of the girls above it, waiting like communicants under their black tarp, light from their candles kindling on their throats and their cheeks. The girl second from the right cocked her head and lifted her chin, as though she was waiting to hear an untenable position defended. To her left, the girl in the white hoodie who looked younger than the rest even though she was the tallest still gazed uneasily into the distance, her mouth open slightly to show a set of rabbity front teeth, her eyebrows raised in apprehension or excitement. Only one of the girls, her bag strap crossed over her chest like a bandolier, looked directly at the photographer. As she stared, her expression seemed to change and the courage I saw in her face appeared to bleed out. She was the sister of one of the Trojan women in that famous painting by Christoforo Reyes which I'd written my undergraduate dissertation on. Reyes, with his exquisitely mannered portraits and court paintings, and whose unfinished epic sequence of which the Trojan women are a part is those court paintings' schizophrenic counterpart, thicked his late paintings with some unspeakable experience into which so many scholars read the record of his service in the Peninsular War. In rabid, reinforced lines, Reyes had painted in shades of ochre and grey three women gripping each other, their hands quietly clawing at each other's wrists. The third woman looks over her shoulder as if expecting to see some horror pursuing her.

The other two wear expressions of growing howls, their eyes wild with the future. Contemporaries of Reyes had judged it barbaric. 'Can art develop backwards?' Schneidermesser, the early-nineteenth-century German art critic, had written to his mistress, baffled. In the twentieth century, Clement Greenberg had called the painting a foretaste of *Guernica*, and so maybe it was Greenberg's fault that the painting was stolen in 1989 from a temporary exhibition at the Cleveland Museum of Art and never recovered. Like the women in Reyes's masterpiece, the Mexican girls in the Reuters photograph stood shoulder to shoulder, suspended in time, waiting for the final breaching of the walls. You can still find them on the Internet: standing as women have always stood, midwives to a history thrust through the slit in their front door.

2

There was only one other friend of mine who knew about the missing students of Guerrero. Helen and I met because she was dating a good friend of mine, although she and Alex have since broken up, a break-up which by all accounts was rough and took several tries while one or the other said or did things they regretted. We had become friends, Helen and I, one night at a dilapidated pub in Stepney called the George, because of our shared love for Roberto Bolaño. Helen's interest was academic as well as personal: she was doing a doctorate in comparative literature at Birkbeck University, with a particular focus on the contemporary Chilean novel, of which Bolaño is the godfather. Unlike me, she read Bolaño in the original Spanish, whereas I could only rely on the translations, published each year until the archives of the dead writer had been entirely exorcised of their ghosts. Helen wanted to be a translator: she wanted, ideally, to live in Latin America, to be Latin American, to know the savageness of life on that other planet. After reading Bolaño's novels, she admitted to me, she found life in London dull and insubstantial. No one talked about art, she said. No one cared about literature enough to steal a book as Bolaño and his friends had repeatedly done, even among her peers at Birkbeck, several of whom were spending a lot of money to pay for their graduate study of Rilke, or Tolstoy, or queer Portuguese writing between the wars. It was something they felt bound to do, something that tired them, which was ridiculous because it would never make them any money, and they ought to have given it up for something more lucrative, like consulting or the law. Helen was able to talk about the dullness and insubstantiality of life in London because her father was a prominent psychiatrist on Harley Street, and her mother was a first violinist in the Scottish Chamber Orchestra, and she was an only child. Her life was beautifully curated, and even though she had been encouraged to keep within a modest allowance by her parents, their evident adoration of her (so my friend Alex, her ex-boyfriend, told me after they broke up) meant that she never encountered any real discomfort. Helen lived enchantedly, so it was only fair that she envied the struggles of the disenchanted, whose scars and whose deprivations made them permanent, multi-dimensional works of art themselves. When you talked to Helen, you had to take her limited frame of reference into consideration. At no point could you point to her privilege, but it was there perpetually, the untouchable subject, like the state of Israel.

Helen was right when she said that no one in London cared about art – though it seemed a strange thing to say with the amount of money circuiting the London art world, and knowing the galleries, the prizes, the radio shows, the documentaries, the underground magazines, the parties in Peckham, Shoreditch, Soho. On the whole, aside from those brief hot-tempered undergraduate rows, when a group of people who professed an interest in art got together, they talked about cocktails, they talked about their holidays. If they made art (sculptures, poems, plays), they talked about their love affairs. Helen, dear posh Helen, was one of the only ones who cared. Yet even Helen, I had no doubt, would marry a banker, would come to do her translations – now her passion, soon an increasingly distant hobby, as the savageness of another planet shrank into nearer obligations – in the time motherhood spared her. Still, it was Helen who mentioned the forty-three missing students, the *desaparecidos*, she called them with only minor pretentiousness, when I saw her at a Christmas party thrown by one of our mutual friends. She had followed the news more closely than I had, because she had actually been to Mexico. And, I pointed out to her, it was Helen who was still a student; she shared with them some form of solidarity. Students were always the first to be thrown under the bus. We maintained our hatred of Nick Clegg with virtuous ferocity.

'Of course they're dead,' said Helen.

Then why call them missing? I asked.

'You've read *Amulet*, haven't you?' she said. 'Don't you remember the poet trapped in the toilet? Mexico has a history of enforced disappearances, particularly students. It still sends people to the streets. It causes protests: serious protests, not just the ones we managed after the tuition fees changed, but real protests where they call in the army. And, of course, the people protesting suspect they might go missing too. You should read Elena Poniatowska.'

I could tell from the increasingly distracted way she spoke that, while she had followed the news of the students more closely than I had, her interest in the subject was fading. She was looking over my shoulder for Alex. As I said, this was in the dog days of their relationship. I followed her gaze and saw Alex drinking conspiratorially with a man I'd never seen. They had that prickly air of men saying things they'd never tell their girlfriends, both briefly and gloriously released from their leashes into something feral. If you happened to catch Alex when he was looking your way, he'd look back at you with the flat yellow eyes of a fox. You can tell by looking at a fox's eyes how the rest of the night will go.

And I was right. I learned later from Alex that they had broken up for good later that night, after the party, and that Helen and Alex both spent the week between Christmas and New Year moving out of their shared flat when the other was out. I'd not seen Helen since, which was a pity because I'd never met anyone who knew so much about Roberto Bolaño. She'd even been to his house in Blanes, Spain, where he lived until he died at the Vall d'Hebron University Hospital in Barcelona. In fact she told me she'd met, quite by accident, a man on the flight from Stansted to Barcelona who had treated Bolaño at the hospital before his death when his regular physician had had a family emergency and had required a substitute to stand in for him. When she had asked the man what Bolaño had been like, he had shrugged and said that the man had really been in very poor health, but that occasionally he told good jokes. The man who had treated Bolaño wanted to recount one such joke to Helen, but in the end he apologized and said he couldn't remember any of them. Helen had tried to find the writer's former house in Mexico City, too, where he'd lived from 1968 to 1973, and then again from 1974 to 1977 – she was one of those people who liked literary pilgrimages – with little success. The local writers she'd met had been tired of being asked about Bolaño.

They were glad he was dead, they told her. Now there might be room for the books they were writing. She told me she hadn't thought much of their books, which seemed derivative or shocking for the sake of being shocking. They had no sense of proportion, she said.

3

In Britain, someone is reported missing every ninety seconds. In Scotland, they say, more people go missing in the spring and summer months than in the winter. According to the figures, children are twice as likely as adults to vanish. When I was in primary school, a boy in my class disappeared. The nuns held their tongues and said nothing. Weeks later, when it occurred to me to ask my mother about Rudy, she said his family had moved away. She didn't have to say why. His older brother had been killed playing in the street after school. The driver of the truck hadn't seen him. He didn't die right away, Rudy's brother. They thought he'd pull through, but in the end there was too much swelling in the brain. I had imagined very clearly Rudy's brother's skull cracking open like an egg on the pavement, its glutinous yellow inner fluid seeping out, like the yellow blood of caterpillars and locusts we crushed experimentally in our back gardens. None of us, Rudy's classmates, ever referred to the tragedy. Seven-year-olds know to keep silent about death, having just discovered their own mortality. Then, when I was sixteen, Rudy reappeared as unexpectedly as he had gone away. If I'd expected his face to be prematurely lined, for his hair to have a streak of white, for there to be some sign of early grief, I was disappointed. Rudy was lively, broad-shouldered, a good cricket player. He quickly established himself as the class clown, an excellent mimic, a flirt. He'd even lost his stammer. It was as if his brother had never been, as if the truck had never shattered his brother's skull, as if his family had never departed in what had seemed to me to be the middle of the night, a move which may well have been planned and might have had nothing to do with Rudy's brother's death.

Like Rudy's sudden reappearance years later, the students from Ayotzinapa came back to me without warning. I was on the Jubilee line going north, well after the two-year internship at *Figura* had failed to turn into a job and I had begun to work at the endoscopy clinic to prove to Nat that I could be pragmatic, that I could pay my share – symbolically at least, if nothing else. I was looking through a copy of the *Evening Standard* abandoned by a man at Green Park and listening to the four or five Spanish students who got on at Baker Street. I could tell they were students by their leather jackets, the guitar slung over a shoulder, the man rolling his cigarette, the girl with tangled hair looking at the photos she'd taken on her bulky DSLR. Film students from Madrid or Barcelona who looked the part, who spent their evenings complaining about London, about the provinciality of the English, about the pubs that closed at eleven, and the grimy weather, and the stodgy, expensive food, but who would go back to Spain and remember the shabbiness of this year abroad with fierce affection for the rest of their lives.

I lost interest in them the second I saw in the *Standard* that the body of Lady Lucan, a woman I'd thought had been dead for the past decade, had just been found in her home in Belgravia. The late dowager countess looked out blankly from her printed photograph, trying to preserve an outline of dignity from her blue armchair, propped stiffly forward so that her hands lay useless, one on her knee, the other on the armrest. The countess's white hair had been brushed into a tentative beehive, but the wisps of hair at her ears and the crooked blue curve of her eye shadow gave her a look of derangement, the frayed composure of an alcoholic housewife. The expression on her face was one of carefully maintained dumbness, of a woman who no longer wished to disturb her companions by asking the questions which forced themselves on her. She had died, the article said, on 26 September of unknown causes, on the same street in Belgravia from which her husband had disappeared forty-three years before. As I read, I felt a scratching irritation that had nothing to do with the tenner I had misplaced at lunch or the sour smell coming from the gym bag across the carriage. It was like a wisdom tooth pressing against the surface of the gum, a tap-tap-tapping through the ceiling from the flat above, the grit an oyster feels which starts the pearl. Lady Lucan annoyed everybody – was that it? – the judge, her sisters-in-law, her husband. It was her exasperating look of the child bride: her perpetual, mournful vulnerability. We cut her out of the story, Nina and I, and liked her only for her blood-soaked shrieking at the Plumbers Arms. We felt sorrier for the dead nanny.

That wasn't it.

At West Hampstead, the students alighted with their Rizlas and instruments and scarves, leaving behind an English silence, a rush-hour silence, in which the exhaustion of the day, the longing to be home, sore feet, wet socks, scratchy contact lenses and evening engagements briefly defeated us. I left the Tube irritably at Kilburn, and on the walk between the station and the flat, passing under the railway, passing the vendors of discounted Chinese plastics and the nail salons and the eyebrow threaders, the acupuncturists and the laundrettes, the Turkish restaurants and kebab takeaways, ducking the smell of rotisserie chicken and exhaust fumes, I picked over the story – the dead countess, the house in Belgravia, the unsolved disappearance, the 26th of September, forty-three years later – and it was only once I turned the key in the door, as though I was turning a key in my memory, that the facts fell into place, as though I'd solved a portion of that other disappearance; as though, having passed this first test, it – or rather they – had chosen me.

4

It's just as well Nat and I had agreed not to speak to each other until after breakfast. In the hours between *then*, when I'd turned my key in the lock, and *now*, as Nat waved at me with the flat of his hand to step away from the kitchen doorway with the authority of a man on a tight schedule towards a woman who would spend the day at home, I'd let yesterday's discovery thicken. Of course, it was pure coincidence that Lady Lucan had died forty-three years after her husband disappeared, on the anniversary of the day on which forty-three Mexican students disappeared. Of course it was. But wasn't coincidence just the word given to a pattern you couldn't yet interpret? All I could say is: I saw it.

Once Nat had wrestled his feet into the shoes he'd failed to properly untie the night before and I could no longer hear his staggering gait on the stairs, I filled the sink with soap and hot water and looked out the window. The window over the sink looked out on to a row of gardens which belonged to the ground-floor flats and on to the balconies which jutted out from the housing estate backing on to their borders. Whenever I washed the dishes, whenever I overfilled the sink so that the tepid water slopped up and left a residue, a stinking mucilage that built up over time so that it now needed a scalpel to clear it, I looked out at the gardens. Through the window, I had seen the next-door neighbours' sons aim at a nest in a tree in their garden and, when it fell, saw them bury the chicks alive in a hole they dug with their hands. I watched the neighbours' dog later dig up the birds and gnaw on their carcasses. I watched the mother of the boys discover the dog and strike him across the head with her shoe. I began to hate them: the boys, the mother, the dog. I didn't hate the man of the house, a sad, gluttonous man who smoked secretly. Once I saw him touch himself while he looked at his phone in the twilight. I was about to lean out of the window to shout at him when it occurred to me that maybe he could not go about his satisfactions within his wife's principality.

When the dishes were done and the sink drained, I picked up the phone to call my mother and tell her about Lady Lucan. But after a few rings I hung up. It was the middle of a school day, after all, and it would only confirm her suspicion that I was living off Nat's greater sense of adulthood. Besides, talking to my mother tended to pick maggot holes in my mind. Nina's brain worked like a spider's web. In term time, she tried to snap off as many digressions as she could, forcing conversation into straight channels, erasing the details it was her nature to hoard in the interest of the efficiency she had been told her role as Head of Department required. I liked her better in the middle of the summer holidays, when she let her instinctive incoherence take over, and we spent hours talking without either of us asking for a definition, and the names we called each other when I was very young – Neenaw and Gee-up, names so babyish they made Nat (who had no nickname) blush – were taken out of their old boxes. She wouldn't understand, in the middle of term, the coincidence of 26 September, or the echo I was beginning to feel was a calling card. I'd start at the beginning, I thought, and it would be as easy as lifting my eyes to the window when I stood at our sink, with its residue and its foul grouting and its coffee stains.

That beginning was not 26 September 2014, I learned when I opened Wikipedia, but October 1968. Because it was the anniversary of the Tlatelolco massacre of 1968 which, at the end of September 2014, had led the students enrolled at a rural teaching college in Ayotzinapa, in the poor dry province of Guerrero, to hijack buses intended to convey them north for the commemorative march in Mexico City. The march observed the anniversary of that tragic autumn of 1968, when, only a few days before the Olympic Games were to be held in Mexico City (an additional pressure no one needed and one which surely contributed to the savagery of the government's actions), students and workers and mothers and children and journalists had gathered peacefully in the Plaza de las Tres Culturas to protest. They had stood between the baroque church of Santiago Tlatelolco, the Aztec ruins which were not yet fenced off, and the Ministry of Foreign Affairs, three colluding barriers which many of the protestors did not register as such until it was too late, when the helicopters circling overheard had set off the flare which signalled to the obscurely white-gloved officers positioned on the roof to begin firing. The uncertainty and confusion of the events at Tlatelolco metastasized, only to be reproduced (so to speak) in tens, perhaps hundreds, of subsequent massacres, as the spiritual sons of Tlatelolco, the sons and nephews and cousins of the white-gloved marksmen, carried out their grim work in secret warehouses, police stations and barracks. If a genealogy couldn't be precisely enumerated, no one doubted that it was on account of that mother of crimes, the massacre of '68, whose fog of disquiet (bred by years of official obfuscation and maladministration) continued to veil those that followed in its wake, among which was the disappearance of the forty-three students of Ayotzinapa. Because of this fog, and because, like my mother, clarity had never been my strong suit (what did I mean by the 'sons of Tlatelolco', for example? What the hell did I mean by 'genealogy'?), I found a notebook in a drawer and tried to summarize what I read to keep me on track, the way children used to wear braces to correct their posture.

Every year at the beginning of October, I wrote, it was the tradition for students from poor, radical, rural teaching colleges like the Escuela Normal Rural Raúl Isidro Burgos in Ayotzinapa, Guerrero, to hijack buses to convey them and their classmates to Mexico City for the anniversary of the Tlatelolco massacre of 1968. By commandeering buses to protest against the government, the students had, admittedly, made few friends among local law enforcement, and there had been previous altercations. On 26 September 2014, the students travelled west to Chilpancingo, the capital of Guerrero and after Acapulco the second largest city in the state, where they attempted to acquire more buses. When they failed, they returned to Ayotzinapa with two vehicles in their possession. Later, they chose to go to Iguala, a city 126 kilometres to the north, in the direction of Mexico City.

There was something improbable about this start, I thought, as I read over what I had written: something out of proportion with the story's end. This amateur thuggery Bolaño could have done something with. He might have described one of the student's first blow job the day before the theft, how he could have quite happily given the entire Tlatelolco circus a miss, only his more zealous classmates (the ones, say, who could recite phrases of Marx word for word, along with certain sentimental paragraphs of Hugo) wouldn't hear of it.

It was in Iguala that things went downhill, I wrote. In Iguala, they got what they had come for, but then the police, or undercover police, or armed men passing for police showed up: unidentified gunmen seen at crossroads and bypasses and the peripheries. Later, after the skies opened, hundreds of spent bullet casings lay uncollected in puddles and gutters, like the abandoned shoes and crushed flowers which witnesses of the earlier massacre remembered clotting the Plaza de las Tres Culturas.

Reports later emerged of five separate attacks launched at various points around the city that night, each of which I copied down precisely, both the time and the location, as I had been trained to do. I copied the facts down the way that art students draw from life – the way that scholars who decipher certain documents written in a difficult hand trace the shapes of the letters until they make sense.

The first attack of the night, I wrote, occurred at 21:30 on the corner of Juan N. Alvarez and Emiliano Zapata, north of the parish church of San Francisco de Asís, where the city's public squares and central park give way to a thicket of telephone wires, telecommunications providers, bars and shops selling statues of Mary and the Virgin of Guadalupe. The second, during which three students were shot and killed, took place almost simultaneously with the first, on

Juan N. Alvarez and the city's broad and dusty ring road, the Periférico Norte, two kilometres north of the first attack, across the river. The third attack took place on the highway which runs almost directly south to Mezcala and is sometimes referred to as the *Autopista del Sol*, the Highway of the Sun, whereas the fourth attack broke out at twenty minutes before midnight when the bus belonging to a football team from Chilpancingo, the Avispones, who had won their match against the local Iguala club by two goals, came under fire. The fifth and final attack took place at the intersection of Juan N. Alvarez and Periférico Norte, as if the first encounter hadn't been enough and the attackers had come back to finish the job they'd started, or as if they'd been given orders to leave no trace behind.

The attacks, when connected, made up a perforated outline, a shadow map of the city, the way stars can be joined to look like certain Greek heroes or animals. Among the six confirmed fatalities of the attacks were a fifteen-year-old member of the victorious but ultimately unlucky Avispones, and the team's driver; a woman who had the misfortune to climb into a taxi later caught in the crossfire; and the three students who were killed in the second attack. The next morning, the morning of 27 September, the mutilated corpse of one of the students, Julio César Mondragón Fontes, was discovered north of the Periférico Norte with his eyes gouged out and the skin flayed from his skull. In addition to the six murders, at least twenty people had been wounded in the ensuing crossfire, seven of whom were students, and forty-three vanished. They were led away by armed men who might have been police, or perhaps soldiers, or even marines, driven away on trucks, and never seen again.

5

At first, it was the flaying that kept coming back to me. I thought about it when I shaved my legs and cut myself on the tricky reef of my ankle. I thought about it when I peeled off a pair of pink rubber gloves after I'd cleaned out the fridge. And when I rubbed brown sugar, chilli and paprika into a ham Nat picked up from the butcher's on West End Lane, I did it quickly and without looking at what I was doing, as though all skinless meat shared some nervous system in common, and Julio César Mondragón Fontes hadn't been in the ground for three years.

'What's wrong?' Nat teased, as he watched me work.

'You do it,' I said, and threw the apron with its patches of pig juice at him.

As an undergraduate, I had sat through a lecture on Titian's painting of the flaying of Marsyas in which the lecturer had drawn our attention to the hand of near-sighted Apollo, doggedly scraping and plucking the victim's skin away from his body. It was a claustrophobic painting, I thought, both frenzied and horrifically calm. The lecturer's glee at the dog licking up the satyr's blood was one more sign that he should take the retirement on which the department was rumoured to be increasingly insistent. Gordon Gearing was a small Australian in a seersucker shirt, with a shock of white hair, a weak chin and sluggish, fleshy lips he nursed between sentences. 'They'll tell you that this painting anatomizes the human spirit,' he'd told us. 'Brutality and beauty. Don't you think he's enjoying himself?' As a rule, Gearing expected his questions to be answered, so someone eventually said, 'Who? The god or the goat?' 'Marsyas, of course,' said Gearing ('The god or the goat,' he repeated, already tucking the line away to rework into an anecdote over dinner). 'If you look at his face, if you get it the right way up, you'll see bliss, believe me. Is it about the triumph of the human spirit? This late vision of Titian's, which several of your leading novelists (*once*-leading novelists, I should say, unless anybody reads Miss Murdoch now), your *once*-leading novelists have read as a commentary on the mysteries of faith. Who's to say? I'd be more inclined to say it comes from sexual frustration, the ancient painter's almost certain impotence – look how much fun there is in Apollo's single-minded scraping, look how *shaggy* it is – that thirsty little dog there – no, this has nothing to do with spirit. It's about appetite. Still,' he said to himself after a pause, 'how many animals arrange their victims before they consume them? How many animals actually enjoy making themselves sick?'

It was one of the only observations in Gearing's lecture that had the ring of truth. Here was savagery as ancient and vicious as scalping or crucifixion, those other blood rituals where death is secondary to the pleasures of form. And it was the flaying of Mondragón Fontes that gave away what must have happened on the night of 26 September. The sporadic gunfire, the skirmishes on street corners, the woman whose luck ran out as she climbed into her taxi: these were signs of some catastrophic collision, clumsily explained away as casualties in a battle for law and order. But the mutilated corpse of Mondragón Fontes said otherwise. Whoever took out his eyes and peeled the skin from his skull had known himself to be the master of his time. The missing eyes were a warning to the people of Iguala to unsee whatever they had seen, or whatever they thought they'd seen. But the stripping of the skin was sheer decadence, Aztec cosplay: infernal graffiti declaring the unleashing of energies that couldn't be called back. The man with the knife, whoever he was, had turned his back on butchery: this was the torturer's art, the prelude to cannibalism. By removing the skin, he made the corpse of Mondragón Fontes a work of art to which he signed his name, like any other artist. And now here I was, another appalled visitor to the gallery, watching its value rise.

6

From a distance, Mexico is a stomach, curving to the right rather than the left, tapering from a wide duct to a narrower passage, the colon through Guatemala, Belize, El Salvador, Honduras, Nicaragua, Costa Rica and Panama, down to Colombia and the continent below. At a certain distance, so far out that everything was visible from Baja California to Houston, and from El Paso to Mexico City, I could see the names you might sing to the sound of a guitar. Navojoa, Torreón, Aguascalientes, Guadalajara. Across the border to the north, the Anglo thud of McAllen and Brownsville, towns that might have been named after local home improvement stores, or the manufacturers of reliable handguns.

The timestamp on the Google Maps image said February 2009, a period when the forty-three missing students of Ayotzinapa were still alive, with no hint of the role history would assign them. They might have been sharing a warm Coke under a roof, waiting for the air to cool. They had more than five years of life left.

I had imagined a provincial structure, cheaply built, with several rooms, a blackboard, low wooden desks and no books, but from the air the Escuela Normal Rural Raúl Isidro Burgos in Ayotzinapa looked as large as a ranch. I saw a series of red rectangles shielded by trees which from the air were nothing more than green clouds. Behind the school was what looked like a large gravel track which, from this height, resembled a rubbish dump. Beyond the college, dry cultivated fields gave way to a vast scrubland veined with a highway and capillaried with side roads winding through it. From a greater distance, I could see that the scrubland and the highway were in the foothills of what appeared to be a mountain range. Time moved according to its own laws. If I scrolled to the left to follow the curve of the mountains, I saw a wall of night growing across Guerrero like a blanket drawn up over a body in the morgue. Night fell on the spine of the mountain and the Escuela Normal Rural Raúl Isidro Burgos, built in the foothills of a range I couldn't name, the natural buffer between Chilpancingo and Tixtla that was about to be drowned in the dark.

At last, I set myself down on the highway, a single carriageway, with the noonday sun above, wild grasses on the hillside, and a dirt lay-by to my right, where the scrub sheltered discarded bottles, bright green wrappers, cartons and torn plastic bags. Between the rubbish and the trees – tall trees, leafy but scraggly, made to withstand heat and drought – I might have been in the Magaliesburg, where Nina and I once stayed with an old boyfriend of hers on our way to Kruger Park, though the detour, which was never adequately explained to me, added considerable hours to our journey. Nor could I see what my mother saw in Johannes, with his placid eyes and his long socks and khakis, his ebony animal statues and the springbok rug in the lounge, thick with the dust of his Voortrekker ancestors, though he told decent jokes and gave me cans of purple Fanta which I drank at the poolside while they (so my mother said) talked. I still find it impossible to imagine Johannes in uniform, or those placid eyes looking out over the mine-strewn fields of Angola. He'd buried his conscripted military service as thoroughly as my teachers had: as he did not think to bury his pioneering past. After the sun set, he drove us out into the veld to see the stars and to hear the baboons bark. I'd been terrified of what lay coiled in the dark, under the rocks, waiting to bite our ankles.

When I retraced my steps back along the highway between Chilpancingo and Tixtla I saw the same vehicles again and again: the maroon Mazda, the white GMC truck with a wheel tied to its roof, the black Ford, the white van with tinted windows. Back and forth on the road, the order of the cars never changed, and the drivers, obscured to me, though I could see the baubles hanging from their rear-view mirrors, never knew I was there.

7

Our door was so old that Regan's knock rattled the hinges. There she stood in a leather jacket and miniskirt, her platinum hair cut like a pixie's, the real kind that hexed your cows and pricked your tyres. A new tattoo climbed up the length of one of her legs in blue and green and pink: creeping plants with flowers reaching out towards the skirt that swallowed them.

'Martha's kicked me out,' she said. 'Cup of T?' She raised a bottle of José Cuervo she was holding by the neck. Nat would be back soon: I was losing my best hour for private schemes, drawing maps, dwelling on grievances, but she couldn't stay outside on the landing.

'Where's our lord of the manor?' said Regan, kicking off her shoes. 'Out with his fellow wigs?' She flopped onto the brown faux leather couch that came with the flat so that I could see her tattoo more clearly. 'Go on, find us some glasses,' she said.

'Is that from a Morris print?' I asked, nodding at her leg. You couldn't tell where the tattoo was meant to start. It seemed to be branching or perpetually dividing and doubling so that the lilac-coloured flowers' wayward petals curled symmetrically, extending into further fronds, into pink blossoms blowing open or drawing together, and into dark green nettles and calyxes – birds too, emerging to sing with their speckled backs to each other and, elsewhere, hunting seed-freckled ruby-coloured fruit.

'I'll tell you what it is,' said Regan, 'it's three hundred quid I'll never see again. And I haven't sold a story in a month,' she said. 'I've got one in the bank but no one's biting yet. I'm working on something bigger.' Regan was always going to be a real reporter, investigating, digging up dirt, getting on people's nerves. I'd met her on the journalism course at City, in the Three Kings on the day her first story was published in the *Guardian*. I'd suspected that the way she'd sat at her table – legs resting on the seat of the chair opposite, head cocked to take in the scene on a tilted axis while pints and chasers appeared at her elbow – had been her style for some time. Despite the story and the drinks, she was bored, and I soon learned that when Regan was bored, she amused herself by pulling the rug out from under other people's feet. Once you were used to her, you knew to turn the tables – it was what she wanted: the stimulation of reversal, of the force that comes from opposition – but at our first meeting, I thought she was a bully for asking Simone Beal, the greasy-haired, sour-smelling daughter of a baron, who was visibly in the middle of a mental breakdown, if the phrase 'too posh to wash', in her experience, had any currency. Regan's careless-ness, the splaying of her doll body across stools and sofas, seemed as exaggerated as the attention the others paid to her. I could feel their peripheral awareness of her, but whether it was the effect of the article or her charred charisma, I couldn't tell. She'd had the sharpened look of a bird on the hunt, of the falcon that hovers in place, combing the brush below for signs of life. When it was my turn to come under the claw, and she asked me if I was a racist (adding, for the benefit of the others, that all South African expats were racist), I said, stupidly, 'What do you mean "racist"?'

'You're in the wrong industry, sugar plum,' Regan said when she'd finished laughing. 'We're not trying to get into the OED. You've got to ask the five questions: Why do you ask? Who said I was racist? When did they say it? How dare they? Where's my lawyer?'

Once the circle had scattered, some to the bar, some to roll cigarettes on the street, she sat up. 'Don't mind me,' she said. 'I'm being a bitch because I was supposed to be on Naxos and I'm in this shithole instead. What's in your hand?' She fluttered her fingers at me in a gesture to hand over the book I was holding. I'd been re-reading Berger's *Ways of Seeing* on the Tube to and from the flat I shared in Elephant and Castle with two girls from Joburg on a gap year who spent most of the money they made from their bartending jobs on molly, and I'd carried the book into the pub as insurance, and, maybe, as a passport.

'Fuck me,' said Regan. 'Margit, you are what is called in the parlance of my people a swot.'

'People read in pubs,' I said, snatching back the Berger and slipping it into my bag.

'Pubs in Cheshire, maybe,' said Regan. 'Or in Arse-end, West Sussex. It's like arriving at an orgy wearing a chastity belt. You might as well wear a neon sign on your forehead that says *I Would Prefer Not To.*'

Regan was older than the rest of us by three or four years and maybe it was this, together with the weight of the *Guardian* story, that made her our godmother. The stories she liked to tell about the period she referred to as her 'wasted years' added up to a kind of loose epic – her affair with a married policewoman in Budapest; teaching English in Dubrovnik; communal living in a decrepit villa in Ischia, where one of the residents was later found to have served time for the murder of his girlfriend's father with the back of a hammer. Somewhere along the way, Regan had come across Flaubert's commandment that to be wild in one's art, one must be orderly in one's life, and did the inverse. Whatever scavenging she did in private, as a journalist she was a meticulous professional, and, just as Jimmy Page must have played his scales when no one was listening, she practised her shorthand, read up on libel law, and never mislaid a business card. When I finally read Regan's *Guardian* story, an exposé of an Oxford college's compromised endowment, I was not the only one who'd wondered if she'd outsourced the writing. There was no hint of her in it, just one substantiated sentence after another. Still, for all her successes, and for all the breadth of her portfolio, she'd yet to find a beat. She liked being a mercenary, she said, a gun for hire.

Now, while I found a pair of clean glasses on the drinks trolley Nat had bought himself when he'd heard he had been awarded pupillage, I asked her what she'd been working on.

'The fishing industry,' Regan said, taking one of the glasses from my hand. 'Possible people smuggling. The industry's crooked enough as it is – Brexit's only made it worse. I went to Harwich for a few days, talked to people, got a few leads.' It was her bottle. She poured and continued. 'There was a white van on me for two days,' she said, 'so I started wearing a body camera to get the registration number. It didn't really bother him – the bastard had tinted windows – so I came back to London. But Martha's finally given up on my bullshit and won't let me back in.'

Martha, Regan's girlfriend, was a child psychologist. When I met her at our engagement party, I was introduced to a woman in a yellow trouser suit with cold hands. Her wedding present to us was a pair of heavy candlesticks, the sort of thing Victorian husbands might use to bludgeon their wives to death. Regan, on the other hand, gave us *Led Zeppelin IV* on vinyl and promised to teach Nat how to ride the motorbike if he ever, in her words, found the stones to ask.

Regan and I knocked our glasses together and drank. It had been ages since I'd traded a bottle back and forth, no ice, no lime, no salt, just business.

'She left me a voice message to say she'd drop my things off at my brother's tomorrow morning and that there was no point in handing over my keys because the locks have been changed, which is fine by me because I lost the keys in Margate. Fuck,' said Regan, 'never move in with a woman who owns her own house – you've got no leverage. Don't worry,' she laughed, 'I'm not going to ask to stay here. I'm going to bother Jim. He's always single. I'll tell him I'll pay him.'

Regan's brother Jim managed the Pale Horse in Brixton, a pub locals called the Mare. His front teeth were once punched out in an attempted robbery and he'd only reluctantly fixed them. He told me once that he liked to remember what it felt like to punch the thief back. The last time I saw Jim his beard had got thicker and longer and his moustache flowed over the top of his mouth like moss on a rock in a river.

'He hates Martha,' said Regan, draining her glass. 'He said

she's always trying to mind-hack him. But she can be generous on her own terms.' She refilled her glass and reached over
to top up mine, knocking over a mug of cold coffee with her
elbow in the process. 'Oh shit,' she said, as the coffee drib-
bled on to the carpet. I waved my hand, watching the sooty
archipelago soak into the calligraphy of the rug. 'It's IKEA,'
I said.

'One day,' she said, 'I'm going to buy one of those winged
armchairs that cost two hundred quid just to put on my roof
and smoke in. So,' she settled back, raising her tattooed leg
and admiring it. It made her other leg look naked, as if she'd
bought them separately and couldn't afford the pair. 'Tell me
about you,' said Regan. 'Life as mamacita.'

In hindsight, I should have kept it to myself. I've since
learned that the early days of an investigation are too tender
for talk, and can easily miscarry. But since there was nothing
else to tell her but endoscopy paperwork and patient lists, I
gave Regan the missing students. I told her about Tlatelolco,
and about the stolen buses, and about the football team who
had nothing to do with it, whatever *it* was. The words rolled
out of my mouth like an unchewed cherry tomato and lay
there on the carpet between us, shining with my spit. She'd
finished her third glass and was reaching for her fourth.

'I thought your beat was who won the Turner Prize,' she
said at last. 'Biennale gossip. Whether performance art counts.
That shit. Stubbs,' she said. 'Now there's an artist. You know
he got horse carcasses from a nearby abattoir and hung them
from pulleys in his barn? Shit, he knew them inside and
out.'

I had a queasy vision of eyeless, skinless Mondragón Fontes
hanging from the rafters.

'What do you think about coincidence?' I asked her.

'You're going to tell me that Nat's parents have just bought you a Stubbs,' Regan said.

'Don't be stupid,' I said, and, since I was already halfway there, I told her about the death of Lady Lucan, a garbled account which began to lose steam almost as soon as I launched into it, not least because Regan, although English, had only a vague notion of who Lord Lucan was. I had to leave the missing students to one side and describe Lucan's gambling debts, his estrangement from his wife and their children, the hiring of poor Sandra Rivett, the nanny, a civilian who through no choice of her own would become a casualty of the Lucans' marriage. I should have stopped there but I didn't. I should have let her go on about Stubbs and his horse paintings, even though I'd never had the slightest interest in Stubbs. I was the only girl in primary school who didn't go through a horse phase and eventually the other girls in my year stopped offering to lend me their Riding Academy books, even *Lessons for Lauren*, which was acknowledged to be the best of them, which is how I spent several years on the fringes of society between the ages of six and thirteen.

But it was no good. I couldn't put into words what I saw: the flaying of Marsyas, the empty ring road, the bullet cases in the gutter, the dusty void of Ayotzinapa. That is, I could say what it was but not what it meant.

The door opened and Nat came in smelling of ale and whiskey, a two-handed habit he'd borrowed from a friend in banking. 'Quick,' he said, pushing past us as we sprawled on the couch and the carpet, and bolted himself in the toilet.

'*Vámonos*,' said Regan, 'I'd better go.' She straightened her miniskirt, capped the tequila and tucked it under her arm.

'Give me a call,' she said. 'Or come to the Mare. Jim likes you. You should see his beard – it's as good as seaweed.'

Then she was off, taking her Morris tattoo with her. Taking her bike with her. Taking her brain and her courage and her small debts with her.

8

It seems like we dressed up all the time in those days. Nat and I met at a Halloween party at a friend's flat in Shoreditch, the year before I met Regan. The flat had high ceilings and large bay windows overlooking the street, and it was a tragic day for all of us when Alice moved to Berlin. We didn't even get the lease passed around – some early-career academic arsehole picked it up, some researcher who never smoked or threw parties, a man who actually washed his shower curtain. Across the street from the flat was an off-licence with an unparalleled selection of what Alice self-consciously called plonk. She said the owner of the off-licence would let her take milk or olive oil or cheese when she was in the middle of cooking on the understanding that she would pay later. She had a gift for picking people up, for poaching them from other parties or mutual friends. Her invitations made you feel genuinely flattered, so that you didn't enquire too deeply into whether her enthusiasm for you was natural. Her memory was good, and that too was flattering. She would remember what you were reading, the projects you were working on, your deadlines. She remembered what you liked to drink, and it was her party trick to mix her guests their first cocktail, no matter how late they were, and her measures were always generous. She liked you to take a sip, make a face, and then tell her how strong it was. She wore a micro-fringe and liked to be scolded.

At this particular party, which took place at a time when I was going to Alice's parties regularly, I'd come as one of Degas's dancers. There were three of us – me, Joanna and Catie – in ballet shoes and tulle skirts, posing for recognition by looking at our feet, or sitting wearily on the floor, stretching our calves. We were asked repeatedly to stand on the tops of our toes, but we were wearing slippers rather than pointes and we got tired of defending ourselves. Later on, when we'd had a bit to drink, Catie did try to stand on her toes, but it was only a few seconds before she fell and ripped a toenail. I knew I looked wrong in that dress. My arms hung down stupidly and I kept snagging my skirt on splinters in doorways and on the edges of Alice's vintage furniture, but I hadn't been able to think of anything else.

Nat came as John Wayne in *The Searchers*. No one knew much about John Wayne except Nat, and we certainly didn't know John Wayne was a white supremacist then or we'd have kicked him out. He had the Duke's height and narrow hips and wore a red cotton shirt buckled into his jeans with yellow braces, and a navy handkerchief tied around his neck. If he'd come with a hat, he'd quickly misplaced it, but he made up for it by staying in character, scattering one-liners as he moved from room to room: 'That'll be the day,' I overheard him saying, and, 'Livin' with Comanches ain't bein' alive.'

We might never had spoken, Nat and I, if we hadn't both been waiting for the toilet. It was far enough into the evening for time to be measureless, and we could have been waiting for two minutes or forty-five and wouldn't have known the difference. I asked him where his gun was.

'No mind,' he said, carelessly, 'I can still whup you to a frazzle.' This sounded like an invitation more than anything else and, as the thought occurred to him, he looked down at me with new eyes from the height of his frontier.

'How much of it have you memorized?' I asked.

'There's not much talking,' he said, modestly snapping his right yellow brace. 'Most of it is riding and shooting.'

'It sounds terrible.'

'It's Scorsese's favourite film!' he said, and I shrugged. 'Says the Sugar Plum Fairy,' Nat said, leaning across the hall and brushing his fingers against my skirt. 'When I wore one of these, it hurt. Doesn't it hurt your breasts?'

I was struck by the oddness of someone my age saying *breasts* rather than *tits*.

'No more than a swimsuit,' I said, putting my hands on the elasticated neck of my leotard, pulling it out slightly, and letting it snap back. 'Do lawmen usually wear tutus?' I said, dragging out *lawmen* in what I thought was an exaggeratedly Southern drawl.

'We be Texicans,' he said. 'Texican is nothin' but a human man way out on a limb.'

I could tell from the way he spoke that he didn't mind the laughter of others. He had not been taught, as other boys had, that being laughed at was a form of degradation. Later in the evening, he was still thinking about my tutu, his fingers on the elasticated band at the neck, following it across my shoulders and down into the dip, brushing across the slick, scaly texture of the fabric. Much later, when I had seen *The Searchers* at least three times, so that it no longer surprised me that when John Wayne finally found Natalie Wood after five years of looking he tried to shoot her, Nat and I went over that first night. He agreed with me: the tutu hadn't suited me at all. Had I thought he was attractive? He was, strictly speaking, good-looking: tall, golden, with even Amish features. There is, I have since learned, sexual attraction in ugliness.

There were so many parties that year – Christmas, New Year, birthdays, bank holidays, Eurovision, parties to celebrate new houses, new degrees, never a new government – that we never had to look each other up. I bought new underwear and wore lipstick; Nat wore cologne and experimented with a five o'clock shadow. At each party, we found ourselves sharing a couch, our inhibitions eroded by the hours. At last, we agreed to see each other on our own. Nat invited me to the Veronese exhibition at the National Gallery, a big, pompous occasion, the art equivalent of a roast dinner, with posters up at every stop on the Underground, and which required advance tickets to jump the long queue snaking out into Trafalgar Square. We went on a Sunday afternoon, when the weather was drizzly and small children in slick, bright-coloured rain jackets ricocheted off the stairs and streaked muddy water like duck shit wherever they went. Nat and I left our umbrellas at the door and walked around the exhibition in that heavy way you do when you've spent money to look at art, pausing at every picture, examining it, squinting at the captions, shuffling to the next picture on the conveyor belt of ancient enthusiasts, edging around men and women with canes and wheelchairs. He regarded each painting seriously, as though he was trying to decide whether or not to add it to his collection.

'You didn't like it,' he said afterwards.

'It was grandiose,' I said.

'You have to see it in its context,' he said, and he talked about the colours, the ways of seeing, the outraged critics. I learned that Nat's taste for art had been formed so thoroughly at boarding school that he'd never break out of it. He had been taught to admire the Italian masters, the Dutch portraitists. He learned to disregard his own instinct and to be fair, thorough, contextual. He knew what he was expected to like: Turner, Velázquez, Bacon. He knew the dates of the artists and the names of movements they were said to belong to. He talked like he had watched BBC documentaries on art with his parents for years, which he had: *Art Before the Revolution*, *Scotland's Lost Masterpieces*, *The Secrets of the Mona Lisa*, etcetera, etcetera. It was then, apropos of Sontag, that I wondered whether he would be any good in bed.

Then again, he had rowed at school, a history I found both exotic and sexually exciting. It had been a landmark in his relationship with his body. It had, his mother told me, taught him to stop slouching and turn his back on fast food, which seemed to have bothered her aesthetically more than anything else. After we'd begun sleeping with each other, Nat showed me videos of his school crew racing at Henley and at training camps in Belgium and the Netherlands, where the rivers were wide, calm and undisturbed. Whatever his intentions had been in showing me the videos, I found myself turned on by them, by seeing the undivided attention he showed to his work, and his utter lack of self-consciousness at being watched as he kept up the continuity of force which flowed from the bow of the boat to the stern and back again.

In time, I discovered other pockets of his personality, the fact that he was encyclopaedic, for example, on the subject of country music. I couldn't discover the node from which this infatuation grew. He had no background in it: no convicts in the family, none of his ancestors had been first cousins, as far as he knew, and he could never really drink cheap whiskey without a sense of determination. I don't know where Nat found the records he listened to – whether his appetite was fed by Reddit forums or vinyl store savants – but he owned it honestly, mocked legacy listeners and never had any patience for Bob Dylan, who, he said, was too much of a troubadour. He lost his temper whenever, in an argument about the merits of the genre, someone brought up Garth Brooks or Keith Urban, who weren't so much second-rate, he said, as committing a form of fraud. He admired albums rather than songs – Willie Nelson's *Red Headed Stranger*, Cash's live recording at Folsom – and though he wasn't deaf to the sentimental charm of Hank Williams or occasional tracks by Townes Van Zandt and David Allan Coe, he had the connoisseur's preference for the forgotten, the overlooked and the undiscovered. His most recent find was a backwoods aristocrat named Campbell, who, after sixty years of hard living, had released two records in close succession. Campbell lived somewhere in Maryland, some kind of reclusive prince palatine whose great-uncle was a famous fiddler and whose aunt was a banjo picker. Nat liked all the stepchildren and second cousins of the genre, except gothabilly, norteña and zydeco. He was as likely to listen to bluegrass as Red Dirt or cowpunk. And he liked books in the first person: Hunter S. Thompson, Bukowski. His early love for Kerouac was fading with time, but he was still soft on him. He wanted to see Big Sur. He was smitten with the myth of the west: road trips, Route 66, motels, tumbleweeds, wide vistas, ranches, spaghetti westerns.

These passions, which I would come to mock and even sometimes despise him for, were also why I stayed. All his formality, his correctness, his politeness and good manners – all the qualities which made me doubt him – disappeared under the dissolving warmth of his enthusiasm, his record collections, the self-conscious bottle of Kentucky bourbon, the harmonica he kept under his bed. I kept them in mind when he gave me improving gifts for my birthday and for Christmas: a membership to the British Museum, a cooking course, a Pevsner guide to the City of London. Behind these gifts I heard a voice: know more, cook more, read more. But I stayed stubbornly thick, attractively (so I thought) ignorant, a fryer of eggs and a scorcher of steaks, whose cakes never rose, and who drank whatever was cheapest. Nat couldn't help knowing what quality was: he couldn't help having a compass of taste pinned to his breastbone, his good manners, his knowledge of what to order and how, just as I couldn't help not knowing. Across the gulf of our upbringings, we made do: I mocked his upper-middle-class perch, and he teased my colonial vulgarity.

There was a time when I could look at him and feel the heating come on. When I had stopped to notice the sum of his features, and felt that his face was the best face I knew. I talked about him as though we were the same person, as though all his memories were mine. I knew how he had slept as a baby, and the first time his friend Simon's older sister sucked him off. I was as indignant as he was at the way his fourth-form history teacher had torn his essay on the Dissolution of the Monasteries into strips because he had written it in pencil rather than fountain pen. If I laughed at him, it was to find some objectivity. When I laughed, I could test our separateness. Familiarity erodes, like a waterfall erodes the stones in the pool it feeds. Maybe teasing, which begins as flirtation, always ends in distaste. Maybe bodies aren't meant to learn so much. The openness of early encounters turns prudish. You begin to dress on your own with the door closed. The only thing that can rescue you is a grand gesture: a spontaneous act of complete generosity. Which of you will commit it? Not knowing, you both wait.

So two and a half years after Alice's Halloween party, there Nat was at his new job, trying to impress the Law Commission, trying to secure pupillage at a reputable chambers, losing his sense of humour, listening forlornly to 'Ramblin' Man' in the evenings. After the internship at *Figura* had finally drawn to an end, I'd applied to the endoscopy clinic at Guy's and St Thomas' to show Nat I could have serious intentions. What could be more serious than endoscopy, during which the innermost organs, suddenly visible, are forced to give up their secrets? The clinic and the occasional weekend shift at the Tate were all I had while I was figuring out how to enter the world of forgeries. Catie, who I'd never been close to, had followed a lover to Chicago; Joanna was awarded a sequence of fellowships which took her to one European city after another; Helen was writing up. Between the long hours at work and his one-night stands, no one saw Alex. And since my visa wasn't going to last for ever, and the Home Office was a rabid den of fox hunters, and there was a small scare when I didn't bleed for two months, Nat asked me to marry him. We were crossing Hyde Park to take a shortcut from Marble Arch to Knightsbridge, where a government minister was holding a drinks reception, and where all the plus-ones were expected to make an appearance, or at least where there were free drinks of the sort of quality you can't afford on hourly wages. The works on the Jubilee line meant we were going to be late if we didn't hoof it, so we hoofed it across the park. This was after the acid attacks, but before the knifings; after the two attacks in Paris but before the attacks on Westminster Bridge and London Bridge and Borough Market; before helicopters seemed to patrol the sky like angry wasps throughout the day, and before everyone was connected to that live wire of fear of dark places, or of public places, of bridges unlined by barriers that took you ten minutes to cross, of lingering at a stop on the Underground. As we walked across Hyde Park, we ignored the sounds from dark corners, the sliding shadows, which were probably teenagers trying their first two-litre bottle of Taurus, or their first joint, or their father's whiskey, their mother's pills. But no doubt in the undergrowth there were also junkies, dealers and neophytes hoping to deal without any fuss; and strangers who'd messaged each other on the Internet to touch each other in person, and married couples out to shake up their habits, and maybe even boys and girls who needed money and chose this as their market for moving up in the world. And no doubt in the thickets there were some wrapped in blankets and sleeping bags bedding down for the night in the spot they knew no policeman would come to, with the ham sandwich still in its packet, saved for the morning. And despite all these secret lives, all our fellows in the park, Nat stopped and showed me the Great Bear and the Little Bear since all the stars I knew were southern stars, and then he asked me to marry him and I said yes, even though he wore glasses, and there is something about men who wear glasses: that moment when you are undressing for bed, when a man takes off his glasses, and his face suddenly looks so unprotected, and you realize with a sinking heart how easy it would be to ruin him, to smash him up.

We married in Grantchester, just outside Cambridge, where his parents lived, and held the reception in Rupert Brooke's apple orchards, an impossibility for anyone else, but not for Oliver and Claudia, Nat's parents, who knew the owners of the orchards and the custodians of the Brooke property, in the casual way such people do.

Now, while he slept off the effects of the ale and the whiskey, his open mouth and muddled breath infecting the air, I crept into bed and waited for sleep to puncture the exhilaration of the tequila and Regan's visit. Regan, who moved through the world as I'd always wanted to: hard, sure, raucous, the kind of person who might be found in a skip one day, or floating in a canal, it's true, but with a resumé that would make her life worth its brevity. After ten minutes of listening to Nat's heavy breathing, I turned my phone over and downloaded a language app. A green owl led me through *el pan, la manzana, la niña, el agua.* It told me cheerfully that my hard work was paying off, even though I was just guessing. Between the sound of trumpets and the slot-machine ring which accompanied this gamble of vocabulary (and still Nat didn't stir), I was shown a boy, a girl, what they eat, what they drink. Their wants were simple: apples, bread, water, milk. The words in boxes moved on, marched in couples, as though people always thought in twos. But who were these boys and girls who drank water and milk and ate apples with such persistence? An Easter chick burst from its egg to shower me with purple badges. After an hour or so, I learned *zapatos* were shoes, not bolts of lightning. I learned *abogado,* lawyer, and *esposo*, husband. *Yo come sólo y duermo sólo.* I eat alone and I sleep alone.

9

My mother's love story, as she told it to me, was straight out of a film, though not a film she'd seen. She was an English teacher in a small town on the coast of the Western Cape, which is known for its surfing, its turquoise lagoons, the occasional shark attack and an easy drugs market. It was a Saturday or Sunday, or maybe just a day in the summer holidays, at the end of 1989 or the beginning of 1990, when the sky was a perfect, uncracked Giotto blue, the stinging blue-bottles arriving as floating bubbles of lapis lazuli only in late afternoon when the tide turned. My mother was at the beach with her friend Melanie and Melanie's brother Thienus, who, despite being at university and several years younger than my mother, tried to impress her. Men did: Nina made an art out of disagreement, and while in my experience men complain to each other about argumentative women, they still liked to have my mother raise an eyebrow at them.

So there she was, young Nina, reading something, if I know her at all, something out of place, like *Bleak House*, something at odds with a South African beach in high summer. Not yet the Head of English at Claremont High, she was just a third-year English teacher who could rest easy in the thought that her syllabus wouldn't have to change or her lesson plans need rewriting. She'd be the first to admit that her intuition about the imminent political change was not very strong, nor did she anticipate the great change only a few years away, although she had marched in Cape Town, she had written letters regularly to the newspaper under her own name repudiating the government's policies, and she had hotly disputed the school's regressive racial stance (which, the governing body reminded her, was the law). Her conscience had not yet prompted her to go so far as to quit, though it gave her some disquiet.

On that day, however, reclining on her towel among strangers, her head full of Lady Dedlock and poor Richard Carstone, she heard a commotion from the water, a froth of foam and waves, and something starting among the beachgoers, a murmuring, babbling unrest. Her friend, seeing her brother was missing, began to fret, not because he was a poor swimmer but because he was thoughtless and more than capable of getting in over his head, which is what had happened. It was not a shark attack, as someone had shouted in excitement. Thienus had gone beyond the red flags which marked the narrow area in which it was safe to swim, and had missed his step, or had come to a sudden drop when the sand bar under his feet had given way, and had panicked and lost his head. He was brought out of the sea twenty minutes later by a lifeguard, who was only a boy himself and had clearly never seen a body before, and an Englishman (as my mother called him) who had been one of the first responders to Thienus's distress.

My mother's friend was beside herself and left with the police who escorted the ambulance carrying the body, leaving Nina behind in the company of the Englishman. The

Englishman, who said his name was Paul, was a man capable of recognizing an opportunity when he saw one, so he took my mother, who was in shock, to the nearest hotel, where the staff of the Kingfisher Bar made a fuss over their beach attire, only relenting when the Englishman handed over a few banknotes by way of intercession. It was there that they drank an unwise sequence of beverages, heedless of the order followed by anyone who wishes to avoid having a colossal hangover the next day: whiskey, followed by beer, a gin and tonic, and then a bottle of Bordeaux. Nina fell asleep at the bar and the Englishman bought her a room. (My father had grounds for being called a gentleman at least once.)

When Nina's guilt over her incidental role in the boy's death had faded, or when she'd lost the will to talk it through, there were fleeting trips to the interior and dawn stalks across the veld. Her discovery that she was pregnant coincided with her discovery that Paul the Englishman was married to a woman in London, where he lived and worked in finance. He had come to South Africa because the banks could sense, as my mother couldn't, the coming change, and had wanted to begin the necessary preparations to thrive in the new dispensation. After more than twenty-five years, the story only made my mother a little angry. But Nina always preferred a good story to a tidy ending. I was seven the first time she told it to me. I don't know if I had asked about my father, or if she had wanted to entertain herself with the strong flavours of past emotion, but I remember the smell of the potted tomato on the kitchen windowsill which she was pinching out as she talked, and the high, green smell of its leaves. Nina said afterwards that, after she'd told me, I drew nothing but sea for the next two weeks: oceans with white clouds of disturbance in the water, but no struggling swimmers, no flailing arms, no bodies. I have no memory of the pictures, but I remember the smell of the tomato plant's leaves, and the milky green of the swelling fruit. I took my father's existence as I took the explanation of sex which came quickly on its heels, as a fact of life. My father hadn't disappeared, because I'd never missed him; he hadn't vanished, because he'd never been seen. Fathers, in my experience, were leathery, ruddy, beery figures, and I envied my friends only when the sun went down after a house in the neighbourhood had been broken into, or when a fuse blew and Nina's experiments with the toolbox collapsed into angry tears. Otherwise, fathers seemed like a kind of unpredictable animal, prodding fires, withholding permission, goaded to perform sudden acts of affection. My father, on the other hand, was like God, whose existence was a matter of metaphysical speculation. He wasn't always pure conjecture; according to Nina, my father was tall, balding, with a sharp dart of a chin and a squash player's leanness. She taught him certain acts of generosity, she said obliquely. She pitied his English wife. From the way he had talked about her, Nina said she imagined a small, disappointed woman who tried to master life's unmasterable wreck. I didn't listen very carefully when Nina speculated on my father's wife; I was as interested in her then as we were in Lady Lucan. But the story of my conception did impress on me the unpleasant but undeniable fact that death makes things happen. Like the tomato's yellow flower – the grave that comes before the fruit which passes through it – death is a constant provocation.

10

It's true that I never thought about them separately, the missing forty-three. They were always a group, each a molecule joined in the chain of some catastrophic chemical compound. Try as I might – to give one the confidence of a lucky birth, a delivery from the umbilical cord around his neck, or another the uncanny ability to guess the starting line-up of the national football team; to wonder if one of the forty-three had had no tolerance for peppers because it aggravated his sinuses, or if another had once longed to be a priest, only for it to come to nothing – it was no good. Like it or not, their fates were bound together, like the members of a crew of Arctic explorers whose ship became trapped in ice. I found their names on a government poster and wrote them in my notebook:

Bernardo Flóres Alcaraz
Felipe Arnulfo Rosas
Benjamín Ascencio Bautista
Israel Caballero Sánchez
José Ángel Navarrete González
Marcial Pablo Baranda

Jorge Antonio Tizapa Legideño
Miguel Ángel Mendoza Zacarías
Marco Antonio Gómez Molina
César Manuel González Hernández
Julio César López Patolzin
Abel García Hernández
Emiliano Alen Gaspar de la Cruz
Doriam González Parral
Jorge Luis González Parral
Alexander Mora Venancio
Saúl Bruno García
Luis Ángel Abarca Carrillo
Jorge Álvarez Nava
Christian Tomás Colón Garnica
Luis Ángel Francisco Arzola
Carlos Iván Ramírez Villarreal
Magdaleno Rubén Lauro Villegas
José Luis Luna Torres
Jesús Jovany Rodríguez Tlatempa
Mauricio Ortega Valerio
José Ángel Campos Cantor
Jorge Aníbal Cruz Mendoza
Giovanni Galindes Guerrero
Jhosivani Guerrero de la Cruz
Leonel Castro Abarca
Miguel Ángel Hernández Martínez
Antonio Santana Maestro
Carlos Lorenzo Hernández Muñoz
Israel Jacinto Lugardo
Adán Abraján de la Cruz
Abelardo Vázquez Penitén

Christian Alfonso Rodríguez Telumbre
Martín Getsemany Sánchez García
Cutberto Ortiz Ramos
Everardo Rodríguez Bello
Jonás Trujillo González
José Eduardo Bartolo Tlatempa

As I wrote, each transcription lit a bonfire, a message rippling up a darkened coast. I wrote as if their names were a kind of code, as though they were behind a thicket, or even a gate, protected by a password, or incantation, which I would discover only in the act of copying them out. And maybe, if I was being honest with myself, I wrote their names less to call them out of hiding than to convince myself they hadn't been invented – by Bolaño himself, say – since every one of their names seemed to call up a fictional detective or police-man, a poet or a boxer, a priest, pimp or assassin. They were names that could have been whispered in the desert. On the official poster, each name appeared beneath a black-and-white photograph of an unsmiling face, heavy with the look of the murderer rather than the murdered, like photos of provincial soldiers a hundred years ago, gauchos in white cotton shirts with red handkerchiefs over their mouths, ready to twirl a Colt .44 around the knuckle and still make their target. Like the victims of all unspeakable crimes, they seemed to wear a look of foreknowledge, as though the second the shutter closed they knew what the photograph would be used for – that they were, in some sense, sealing their fate.

11

I've never been very good at maps, having the unshakeable belief that whatever direction I am facing is north. London is a city that turns on its axis every so many minutes or hours, so that streets which you see plainly with your eyes are parallel or perpendicular take sudden turns or swivels, pivoting or dribbling away in unexpected directions. You take a side road when you come to a dead end, but you shouldn't trust the side road any more than you do the street. Before you know it, you're in another neighbourhood and your greatest conviction – that you are closer than you think to your destination – is disproved by the blinking blue dot that is your lost beating heart.

Sophie Calle, I suspected, never got lost leaving Bond Street station, never stumbled around Mayfair, trying South Molton Street with its espresso bars, where men with slicked-back hair, fragrant beards and beautiful suits smoked and talked real estate. I discovered Calle not on my art history course, but through my old fellow Degas dancer, Joanna. Joanna had scored such a high first-class degree in our final exams that she had gone on to do graduate studies in New York and then Paris without it costing her a penny. It was in our second year, I think, that Joanna had lent me her copy of Calle's *Doubles-jeux*, which she had acquired in a limited English edition published in 1999 by a small, exclusive London press. She told me to read *Venetian Suite* and *The Hotel* which, according to Joanna, were Calle's best works. She also told me to ignore everything in the book by Paul Auster who, Joanna said, was a second-rate author, at any rate second to his ex-wife, the short-story writer Lydia Davis. I didn't care much one way or the other about Paul Auster or even about Lydia Davis, and once I had read *Venetian Suite* and *The Hotel*, I wasn't all that sure about Calle either. Calle's pursuit of a man she'd met at a party in Paris, a pursuit that took her all the way to Venice, was Not Art, I thought, that was for sure. I was prickly about the question of art's self-importance – such accusations were regularly lobbed at us whenever we fraternized with students of economics or history or physics – and Calle's work struck me as the theatrical restlessness of a certain strand of French neurotic trying to dress up her ennui. The more time passed, however, the less sure I was; or rather, I saw that the question might be irrelevant. Either way, when it came to Art, Joanna was nearly always right. After several years of six-month fellowships and zero-hours teaching contracts, and after she had moved from Milan to Amsterdam to Zurich and then, unhappily, back to Paris – a weightless kind of living that sounded chic but also unstable – Joanna had just signed a contract for a one-year teaching job at Queen Mary. *Come to the Connaught Bar*, she texted. *It's time to rip a few more toenails.*

The problem was that, after exiting the tube station at Bond Street and continuing on to Davies Street, I had turned left on South Molton Street. Then, rather than correcting my mistake by taking the next right, I had turned left again where South Molton Street fronted Brook Street, passing the buildings where, in the bricolage of time, Handel and Hendrix had lived side by side. When I reached the palms of Hanover Square and stood opposite Vogue House, where all the young assistants dreamed of macarons, I looked at Google Maps and saw the tangle I'd made. I crossed the street, retracing my steps with increasing haste, since I was already more than fifteen minutes late, and when it seemed almost certain that I couldn't rely on this being the only tangle I would walk into, I found myself standing in front of the gates of the Mexican embassy.

The shock I felt was both distant and familiar: the feeling I'd had as a child of wetting myself, that surprise that what should be kept in was leaking into contact with the external world. Only now I felt the sheer relief of it and none of the shame. I'd begun to feel as though Mexico was an imaginary country, as unreal as Middle-earth; as if the students' disappearance was a tragedy I'd invented all on my own, embellishing it with elaborate histories and fragments of biography, the way children do to make their invented worlds more credible to themselves. But here it was! It existed. The embassy fluttered its green, white and red flag in welcome: it rippled in the sunlight that had just then split the clouds, like a long-awaited castle lowering its bridge across the moat. Then again, I thought, as the clouds regathered and pulled a tarpaulin across the sun, standing outside the Mexican embassy felt like waiting outside the gates of a graveyard watching the burial of a stranger through the bars. Inside the embassy itself, I imagined, the diplomatic staff were doing their daily work of granting visas, answering correspondence, scheduling dinners, banquets, receptions, conducting trade negotiations, making phone calls, filling diplomatic pouches, and perhaps, from time to time, responding to the odd death in unusual circumstances of a Mexican national on British soil, or the occasional repatriation of a corpse.

For a long, seductive minute, I thought about ringing the bell to the embassy or to the consular service next door and insisting at the front desk on a meeting with the ambassador. I'd stride into his office and, since I imagined him sitting with a telephone receiver to his ear at an enormous desk covered in ornate photo frames and ugly gifts from heads of state, I'd order him to hang up the phone. I'd demand that he disclose the current state of the Iguala investigation, and would refuse to be put off by his diplomatic evasions, his accusations of incivility, his insistence that such things had nothing to do with me, his threats to cause reciprocal havoc by calling the British ambassador to Mexico, if not the police. Then again, I thought, Joanna was waiting for me. What's more, I didn't know the Spanish for 'I insist'. The ambassador would be fluent in English, surely – he was nothing if not a professional – but indignation landed better in the recipient's mother tongue.

Reluctantly, I continued down St George Street, casting one last look in the direction of the flag, which was furling and unfurling itself like a sinuous hand which, depending on how you looked at it, either gestured for you to approach or warned you to keep away. Still, I thought as I passed the back doors of Sotheby's, this was another coin in my purse, like the jewellery box I had come across at the charity shop on the Kilburn High Road when I went hunting for wine glasses to replace the ones we'd broken. The jewellery box was nothing more than a cheap trinket kept under the glass at the till, someone's abandoned souvenir. Across its lid in capital letters it read MEXICO, not AMSTERDAM or NEW ORLEANS or even MURANO, but MEXICO, spelled out in imitation mother-of-pearl. As ugly as it was, it had had the air of a relic, a memento mori, and under its influence I had left the shop immediately, forgetting the glasses which were the reason, after all, that I had gone there in the first place.

12

When I arrived at the Connaught, I found Joanna sitting
with a group of women on a curved and conspiratorial green
leather couch which hugged the corner of the cocktail bar's
central section. She was in the middle of a story when I
arrived, so I borrowed an empty slipper chair from the next
table, dragging it as quietly as I could across the writhing
islands that made up the carpet. Joanna was explaining
why she had chosen the Connaught, which, let's face it (she
lowered her voice), was slightly stuffier than the places she
usually liked to go. She liked pop-up bars and dives, she said,
places that were like speakeasies but didn't call themselves
speakeasies. In one sense, she said, it felt right to celebrate
a big occasion properly, like the adult she had to begin to
be, paying council tax and utilities, etcetera. But really, she
continued, she had chosen the Connaught for sentimental
reasons, or perhaps more accurately, for reasons of revenge.
Until recently, as some of us but not all of us knew, she had
been in a long and torturous relationship with a man she
thought she might marry, even though she'd never thought
of herself as the marrying kind. The man was German, a
businessman, neither of which were qualities she'd considered

attractive before she met Christian. He was more conservative than her previous boyfriends, she said, and was very interested in willpower, which perhaps she should have taken as the first warning sign. In hindsight, she said, she probably also should have noticed something was off when he told her that his favourite novels were *The Great Gatsby* and *Bel-Ami*.

Louise, who worked in publishing, observed meaningfully that both novels were very short.

Christian had always promised to take her to the Connaught, Joanna continued, looking over her shoulder to the display of tiered spirits behind the bar which, with its mirrors and mounted crystal serving trays, gave the impression of a cabinet made of ice. Christian had told her it was one of the best bars in the country, she said. This promise, like his promise to introduce her to his family, or to give her a set of keys to his flat, had been left unfulfilled.

To fulfilment! we said, and raised our glasses. *To independence! And paying for your own damn drinks.* The drinks at the Connaught cost three times more than my hourly rate of pay at the clinic, so I drank my Fleurissimo slowly, trying to roll the musked, champagney taste of luxury over and under my tongue. I imagined the pounds slipping down my throat like pearls, one by one.

The pregnant woman sitting across from me introduced herself as Joanna's older sister, Milly. I'd met Milly once before in a state of violent intoxication after she discovered her boyfriend cheating on her, but it didn't seem worth reminding her of how she'd flailed to Fleetwood Mac's 'Go Your Own Way' and then collapsed on the couch saying that she'd never, never, never forgive Luke for making her have to get tested for AIDS. Now here she was, freckled, fecund, sitting with the quiet, rippling satisfaction of a woman who had arranged her life as she might arrange water lilies in a bowl. The other four women were friends from different quarters of Joanna's life: Louise, her flatmate, or rather her landlord; Annabel, a friend she'd made in New York who now worked in London; Justine, a researcher at the Courtauld who sat on a slipper chair to my left; and a new colleague of Joanna's at Queen Mary, a philosopher named Parva who said she worked on something called negative ethics. Negative ethics, she said, could be divided into three strands: disbelief, non-compliance and resistance. Parva parted her long, dark hair in the middle and wore it loose and Ophelia-like to her waist, and the effect was of an undergraduate rather than a tenured philosopher, jarring with the seriousness, or perhaps the philosophic nature, of her expression.

Despite the green leather couches and the sound of the bartenders chipping at a modernist slab of ice or shaking their cocktails like ferocious maracas, and despite the fact that every time I moved my drink and left a smear of condensation a waitress appeared to wipe it away, the force of the embassy hadn't entirely faded. In fact, the more I drank of my cocktail, the more the impression the embassy had left on me developed and deepened, like a cyanotype exposed to strong sunlight. In my mind, I could see again the gate partially opened; the flag fluttering in the sporadic shafts of sun; the ambassador at his desk with the old-fashioned receiver to his ear. The encounter was beginning to take on the significance of a face seen in a dream, and then met again by chance on the street, or side by side in a café.

Meanwhile, Annabel, to my left, seemed to have a way of sitting and listening while other people talked without looking bored. 'What do you think about coincidence?' I asked her. Conversation in the round had dipped when Joanna stepped outside to answer a phone call from her parents and there was nothing else to bind the five of us, although the prestige of their respective positions seemed to draw Parva and Justine to each other, and Milly and Louise had dutifully begun to exchange notes on their calendars: Milly's due date, Louise's upcoming work trip to Munich.

'Coincidence?' Annabel asked. Something about the way she sat and sipped her drink made me think of white culottes, private tennis coaches and pitchers of Long Island iced tea.

'Yes,' I said, 'does it mean anything? Does it matter?'

(The Mexican flag furled and unfurled.)

Parva, who had been saying something to Justine about the fickleness of first-year students, became very still and I could tell she was listening to our conversation. While Annabel was scraping together her answer, Parva leaned forward so that the sheet of her hair slipped over her narrow shoulder. 'It depends how you define it,' she said. 'Jung would argue that some cases of coincidences are chance groupings and others are examples of synchronicity.' Then, since neither Annabel nor I appeared to object to her interruption, Parva added that the difference between chance groupings and synchronicity could be illustrated with one of Jung's own examples. In his lecture on the subject, the eminent psychologist (we couldn't call him a philosopher, she said) had remarked that on a particular Friday, which was also the first of April, he, like many other Germans (or rather German-speaking Swiss, interrupted Louise), had fish for lunch. On the same day, someone – his housekeeper perhaps – had made a passing reference to a European habit of celebrating April Fool's by covertly sticking a paper fish to someone else's back. Later, Jung had happened to make a note about a Latin inscription which contained the word *piscis*, and, in the afternoon, a former patient dropped by unexpectedly, proudly exhibiting to Jung a piece of embroidery she had made which included several extremely detailed and realistic representations of fish. What's more, the next morning, one of Jung's patients had described a dream she'd had in which a fish leaped out of a lake and landed at her feet. Meanwhile, and unknown to most of his friends, Jung was involved in a profound study of the fish symbol, which he'd hoped would feed into his work on archetypes.

Joanna returned as Parva was talking, and I saw that her hair, which she had cut short since I last saw her, had lost its old electric redness.

'In fact,' Parva continued, 'in a footnote, Jung noted that while he had been writing on the banks of a lake, as he set down his pen, he happened to come across a dead fish lying on the sand. He thought all of this was chance, by the way: not meaningful chance, but just a chance series of events, connected only by his mind's attention to, its obsession with, fish.'

Synchronicity, on the other hand, she explained, according to *Jung* (she emphasized his name to distinguish his views from her own), was an example of an acausal event – that is, one removed from the laws of cause and effect – and could only result from an archetypal connection with the individual's unconscious.

'So, when my sister Carrie married a man with the same name as Dad,' said Annabel, 'was that an example of chance or synchronicity?'

Out of the corner of my eye, I saw a man wearing a white

bathrobe and bath slippers appear in the doorway and then take a seat behind the wall that divided the bar into its three discrete sections.

'Jung would say that was chance,' said Parva. 'Like the fish. Like when Ed took me to see Marx's grave in Highgate Cemetery, and it happened to be the same day as the publication of *Kapital*.'

'So,' said Justine, 'let's say you're short of money and sell some of your books. Your local second-hand bookshop offers to buy a few, including a book on impressionism. Your father comes to visit you and, because you can't think of anything else to do, you take him to the bookshop. Later, you find him standing in line to buy a book, which happens to be the book on impressionism you sold to the shop. Is that chance or synchronicity?'

Justine's voice, I noticed for the first time, had a subterranean architecture to it, a European softness to its consonants, an unpredictable openness to its vowels.

'You're bound to have a few interests in common with your father,' Louise objected. 'For all we know, he took you to museums every weekend until you were eighteen.'

In the corner of the room, a black-waistcoated bartender stood at a wheeled drinks cart like a street magician, pouring liquid in a ribbon from his outstretched right hand while the left encouraged its descent. The woman whose drink he was making, a large woman drinking alone, filmed the performance on her phone.

'What about this,' said Annabel. 'I went to Brighton last month, right, and at the end of the night, on the way back to the station, my friends and I stumbled on a group of people waiting outside a little store.'

'An off-licence?' said Louise, who liked to be specific about such things.

'Sure,' said Annabel, who didn't. 'But there was something weird about the way the people were standing: kind of passive, but tense at the same time, if you know what I mean. Then we heard screaming coming from one of the flats above the street: a girl screaming something like *Get off me! Get off me!* It sounded really bad, like, it sounded like she might have been defending herself, or maybe she was just having a breakdown. We couldn't hear everything she was saying so we were listening really hard, and there were more and more people stopping in the street, and people on the balcony opposite the flat (although we had no idea which flat it was coming from), people on the balconies above coming out and straining their eyes and trying to see in and report to us below. It was very *Rear Window.* Anyway, eventually my friend Tim called the police and the police took our details and told us we didn't have to wait. So we continued walking to the station, and because I probably wouldn't have called the police if Tim hadn't been there, we talked about the bystander effect, and we talked about it the rest of the way to the station which, if you know Brighton, is on the top of a hill. When we got to the top, we saw that the café opposite the station was called the Bystander Cafe. The Bystander Cafe! How do you explain that?'

'It's still chance,' said Parva. 'From my point of view, coincidence is far less interesting than contingency. Coincidence is essentially trivial.'

There was a sourness in the air for a minute as the five of us tried to work out whether Parva had just said that we were trivial, and then Joanna intervened.

'I don't think Parva's saying we have to buy Jung,' she said. 'We like patterns, don't we, whether we've invented them or not.'

'But we don't *ask* for things to happen,' I said, thinking of Lady Lucan. 'You might as well say that the patterns in classical music, in Bach, are products of our wanting to find them, when they are part of the structure of the composition.'

'Doesn't that presuppose a composer?' said Parva. 'Are you telling us we have to believe in God?'

'What about Pollock?' asked Justine. 'Are there patterns in *Pollock*?'

'If a man's accused of his wife's murder,' I started to say, putting down my drink, but the conversation was beginning to splinter, once, twice, into cross-currents, reconfiguring its magnetic field into contrary poles. 'If a man's accused of his wife's murder,' I tried again, and then gave up, which was just as well, because I'd forgotten the second clause. Later, on the Tube from Green Park, afraid that I would miss my stop or wander on to a train going in the opposite direction, I kept myself alert by thinking about the way Parva said the word 'trivial', the quick parting of her lips revealing a flash of her pearly, philosophical teeth. I got out my notebook, which I had begun to carry with me wherever I went, and a pen. If you were to draw a diagram of contingency, I thought, it might end up looking like this:

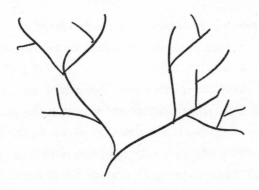

It was a tree of branching possibilities or, rather, an, enormous root system, each forked line representing a fracturing of futures. Instead of trying to raid the city for buses that fateful night, I thought, the students could have gone to Iguala the next day; or they could have given the commemorative march the slip; or they might have been stranded with a flat tyre outside Apango or Mezcala; or, finding themselves under fire, all the students might have managed to make their way through the dark and the rain to shelter in the hills outside Iguala.

Coincidence, on the other hand, would look more like a series of overlapping shapes, a work by Sonia or Robert Delaunay:

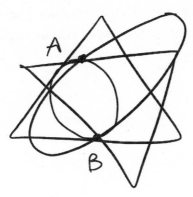

Looking at what I had drawn, I saw a map of the attacks that night in Guerrero. Not a representational map, obviously, but an intuitive, if chaotic, reproduction of the events that had taken place. I labelled two points of connection – A and B – as I had once labelled the geometric figures I drew during end-of-year exams, sitting at one of the desks placed in rows in the assembly hall of my secondary school: figures which were never my strength and which always lost marks for the most insignificant mistakes. The point I had labelled A was, I saw, the overlapping point of the second and fifth attacks, both of which took place, several hours apart, on the intersection of Juan N. Alvarez and Periférico Norte. But I had no idea what point B represented: B was the connection between the thousand unknown factors, between the students and the police, or the students and the mayor, or the students and the mayor's wife, or the students and the army, or the students and the cartel, or the students and several cartels; and the Tlatelolco massacre was a factor too, and somehow the Lucans were a factor, however peripheral, in the same way that the jewellery box and the Mexican embassy were peripheral factors.

There was no point in writing a manifesto, I saw. I couldn't convince anyone that all these tributaries emptied into the same river. I could only track them, one by one, and add them to the map.

13

Nat wasn't thick. He knew I'd started *Breaking Bad* again from the beginning. When he logged on to Netflix or Prime, he could see I'd watched *Traffic* and was halfway through *Amores perros*. He saw *The Savage Detectives* on my bedside table, its stiff spine wrinkled from resisting the coming break. Still, when, one rare Friday night with no champagne reception at his chambers, no beers with Will and Harry, no cocktails to cheer his fellow pupil Liv, no boiler crisis to sort out in his sister Carmella's flat in Dulwich, I suggested watching *Cartel Land*, he asked no questions. There was a twist in his mouth, some small sign of bad wiring – the face people wear when they think you might be eating too much, when their distaste wrestles with their tolerance. But he wouldn't stand in my way, not after he made me watch the *Dollars* trilogy and muttered Eastwood's lines along with him. Now, as we watched, I tried to surreptitiously pick up any clues I could from the lay of the land, from the sunrises and desert sunsets, from the men with their vests and their ammunition. Something in the way Nat and I were sitting reminded me of being twelve, when my best friend was the girl who lived next door to the house Nina rented for us on the edge of a

Cape Town suburb. For a few months, each Sunday, Claire took me with her to church, a plain box of a building without paintings or columns or stained-glass windows or even a pulpit, which is how, until then, I had expected churches to look. The congregation liked to sing, to clap their hands, and, after a long sermon, to kneel and cry and sometimes faint. I went because I liked Claire and because I liked her parents, who let us have sweet *vetkoek* for breakfast. As we sang and clapped, as we sat through the hour-long sermon which sounded to me like the same speech each week but with different Bible stories, I could feel Claire watching me out of the corner of her eye, hopefully, expectantly, waiting for me to give in. I let myself fall down once to see how it felt but I couldn't bring myself to raise my arms or speak in the tipsy shadow language that broke out from time to time. Now here I was, like Claire, watching Nat out of the corner of my eye, waiting to see if he could feel the Spirit.

When the credits rolled, I asked him if he knew that thirty thousand Mexicans had been officially classified as missing. He didn't seem to hear me, but rather continued to scroll through Amazon Prime's stream of comedies – *Frasier*, *Seinfeld*, *Peep Show*, the box sets passing like the wagons of a freight train through a provincial station. It wasn't until a day or two later as he sat down next to me when I started *Sicario* that he delivered his opening remarks. 'I'm sensing,' he said, 'a theme.' On screen, Emily Blunt peered through the punctured plasterboard to see the bloodied shrink-wrapped corpses stashed in the walls; they lined the corridor like saints in a catacomb, bowing their veiled heads in pity. 'Chandler AZ House of Horrors', read the caption on the CNN broadcast before the camera panned away, '42 bodies discovered'. In my notebook I wrote: *Quick-builds? Abandoned lots?*

'What's in the notebook?' Nat said. We watched a plane's shadow passing over mountains which rose and cracked like loaves of sourdough. In Ciudad Juárez, hocks of ham that had once been human hung from an overpass. They twisted like Christ between the thieves.

The next afternoon, I lay on my belly sketching a portrait of Julio César Mondragón Fontes, thinking that if George W. Bush could come to some conclusions while painting portraits of the soldiers he had sent to their deaths, I might as well try something similar. As if a clue would come to me like those billion-year-old comets you only see when you're looking away from them. While I drew, Nat came up behind me and, bending down, planted kisses along my spine like hot stones, one heavy pebble after another laid tenderly from my tailbone to the crux of my ear.

'I'm working,' I said, when I recoiled at the prick of his mouth under my ear. Nat pulled away and, after a moment of studying my sketch, said, sourly, 'He looks nothing like the picture.'

I looked at the photograph of Julio César Mondragón Fontes and then back at my sketch. I wanted to explain that I was trying to undo the image I had seen when I had googled the mutilated man, and which had stuck in my head: the blistered red-black skull left to crack in the daylight, the holes where his eyes had been, fragile as an empty egg carton, the toothy leer of his lipless mouth. I'd had to set my breakfast aside and walk up and down the street to settle my stomach.

After dinner and half a bottle of wine, I decided to hand over my notebook. I watched Nat turn the pages with what seemed to me to be a professional coolness, pausing from time to time over the summaries, making his way across the maps, skimming my lists of verbs, their conjugations and declensions.

'Is this an outsider art thing?' he said at last, holding up the diagrams I'd drawn of contingency and coincidence. 'Are you and Patty putting on some kind of archival exhibition?'

'Don't be ridiculous,' I said. He looked at me for a moment and then, looking back at my notebook, turned a few more pages before flipping back to the beginning. I waited for him to say, 'This is not the way to go about it' or, 'Let's sign you up for proper Spanish lessons' or, 'My uncle Phillip worked in Mexican energy for a few years.' I even expected him to say, 'Explain it to me' or, more aggressively, 'Defend yourself.' And then I could tell him my theories of disappearance as a problem of composition more than anything else, and explain that, like black holes, they pull everything in. I had other theories too, looser theories, about the possibility that attention is a kind of developing agent, like the combination of chemicals that coax a visible image out of film submerged in a tray in a photographer's darkroom: that it makes certain things appear, that it calls something – a kind of responsive consciousness – into existence. The way that, when you look at a dog for long enough, either from close up or from across the street, it seems to become conscious of your attention, becoming restless or, meeting your eyes, beginning to thump its tail against the pavement. And I thought that remembering might be a form of this attention in an expanded or extended form, one that works less in space (like the dog across the street) than it does in time. Remembering might be a kind of fertilizer, if I could put it like that, as well as a preserving agent, giving the past a tongue, or maybe a frequency on which to transmit its messages. But these theories were still under development: I hadn't fully worked them out yet.

'It's your life,' Nat said, and tossed the notebook back to me.

14

Whenever a woman is murdered, everyone knows that the first suspect is her husband. It only stands to reason that when a group of young troublemakers goes missing in suspicious circumstances, one should look to local law enforcement. The mayor of Iguala, I learned, hadn't done himself any favours. As a property developer who'd made his money in the gold and jewellery business, it would have been strange if José Luis Abarca Velázquez *hadn't* made any enemies. Aside from the isolated claims of tainted money and unorthodox investments, there were several disagreements with local unionists and community organizers that went sour; bodies turned up from time to time, as did improbable accounts of Abarca and his shotgun. The mayor's acquittal in the courts wasn't necessarily an exoneration in the eyes of the citizens of Iguala and its neighbours, and any suspicions that may have fallen on Abarca were made worse by his wife. María de los Ángeles Pineda Villa had the misfortune of having two good-for-nothing brothers join the Sinaloa cartel and then its offshoot, the Beltrán-Leyva gang. The fact that both were found dead at the side of the road five years before the events of the night of 26 September 2014 did nothing to dampen the speculation. You can't choose your family, their sister must have said; but if her husband's enemies thought one narco in the family was a misfortune, two was carelessness, and no one believed Pineda Villa was as ignorant of her brothers' affairs as she claimed. But far worse than her connections, Pineda Villa made the mistake of being pretty and ambitious: a short, showy woman with strong eyeliner and a pointed jaw. It was widely supposed that she had her sights set on her husband's job and had been tipped by their party, the Partido de la Revolución Democrática, as his successor. The community event scheduled for the night of 26 September had as its centrepiece a speech delivered by Pineda Villa, ostensibly as the chairwoman of the National System for Integral Family Development, a charity founded in 1977 by the wife of President José López Portillo, and closely associated with the Office of the First Lady: that is, it was an outlet for ambitious and understimulated women on the fringes of power. The size of the event suggested it was far more than a routine annual report, however, and it was widely touted as her formal political debut – the launch of her campaign for the mayoralty.

Shortly after the students disappeared, the whispers had started: rumours that Pineda Villa had been warned that the students were planning to disrupt her event, and that she in turn had passionately urged her husband to act to safeguard their interests. The rumours must have reached Abarca and the First Lady within the week, because by the first of October the couple had gone into hiding. Even if they hadn't been involved in the disappearance of the forty-three students, their own disappearance was an act of supreme stupidity since it only strengthened the presumption of their guilt. Even I could see how bad it looked. By November, the *Daily Mail* was publishing articles with headlines like: 'The bloody rise of Mexico's First Lady of murder: Beautiful but utterly evil mayor's wife who "ordered" massacre of 43 students was the "Boss of Bosses" for cartel behind TWO HUNDRED killings and disappearances'. Regardless of how closely Pineda Villa resembled Lady Macbeth, by late October – a month after the students disappeared – the couple were officially charged with being in league with a local cartel, Guerreros Unidos, an offshoot of the cartel to which Pineda Villa's brothers had once conveniently belonged. In early November, in somewhat disputed circumstances, the mayor of Iguala and his wife were discovered, or betrayed, and taken into custody.

15

According to Google Maps, the road between Tixtla and Iguala takes an hour and forty-nine minutes by car. *VICE* magazine, which covered the missing Mexicans with more tenacity than the legacy broadsheets that looked down their noses at it, reported that the students left the bus station in Iguala at 21:30 on the night of their disappearance. When I dropped in via Street View at Iguala's Central de Autobuses, I was startled to find that instead of being a dark September night in 2014 – as it was perpetually in my mind – the winter sun was broadly slanting the streets. It was November 2009: four years, ten months and six hours before the night in question.

I'd imagined the bus station would be something like Heathrow's, with a dingy roof overhead, and screens showing departures and arrivals – and delays, if it came to that. Instead, there were narrow partially paved streets, with vehicles parked haphazardly over the kerbs, street vendors under umbrellas, pedestrians (it was a weekday, surely), and telephone wires tangling above, and shop signs and baroque billboards in gold-rimmed Spanish black lettering that I associated with tequila, and vegetables spilling out of truck beds, but no clues, nothing for me to conclude except for the centrality of the Central de Autobuses to Iguala life. As I crept around the corner from De Salazar to Hermenegildo Galeana (no English streets had such music, that dash of lizards along the verge, pulpy flowers growing through the stones), I found the bus depot, bare of vendors and walkers, the buses all neatly parked behind a chain-link fence like drugged elephants in a cage. A guard, portly, capped, on the take maybe, was caught in the act of raising his hand.

It was like this, I thought as I lurched down the streets of Iguala, that the endoscopists at the clinic made their way through the pink labyrinths of their patients, confined to the camera's narrow grooves, scanning the footage for signs of disturbance. Not that I ever saw the process itself, stuck behind a desk at reception with Joan and Sarah for the eight or so hours a day patients checked in, checked out, filled in forms and received their referrals, but I'd looked up the process on YouTube when I was first hired, sliding through folds and webs which had the gaudy, glistening curves of a Saint Phalle. Every time a patient came up to me to inform me of their blood sugar levels, or to ask how many consultants were on the ward, or to demand how many more hours they would have to wait, I couldn't help imagining the slick Gothic corridors beneath their clothes, under their skin. They didn't help their case, giving us earfuls about our inefficiency, our callousness, our sluggish disregard of time, since they, the patients, could see us sitting, unhurriedly, hour after hour, playing games with their nerves while they sat in the waiting room with cancer in their bowels.

We saw it all from the front desk: the rabbi reading the *Mail*; the nervous bachelor rubbing his nose with his knuckles; the second wife clutching her husband's things to her lap; the type 2 diabetics, uneasy in their new bodies. Every visitor longing for the embarrassing ritual to be over, and to sink their teeth into a post-procedural chop, salmon fillet or scone with the relieved conviction of having earned it, but still the bubbling dread of the possible unwanted guest in the tunnels within would persist. In the meantime, if they weren't arthritic, they knitted or texted friends with the tips of their index fingers. Over tea and biscuits, my colleagues shook their heads at the hopeless cases who couldn't face a little procedure without going to pieces. Because everyone we saw went into the consultants' rooms, one after another, and they all survived it, in one way or another.

16

On Wednesday, my day off, I set out for the Mare. Perched on the corner of Selborne Street and Cowdray Road, the old pub refused to tart itself up with wooden floors, or black-and-white pictures of what Brixton used to look like in the 1900s, or slogans on a chalkboard outside. The picture of a horse's head hanging above the door was so scoured by the elements that you could hardly tell it was a horse at all. Inside, an aged beige carpet still licked the floor, and the rough assortment of tables and chairs looked as though they'd been scavenged from the dregs of estate sales in the Midlands. There was no Wi-Fi, no website, no food, and the condom dispensers in the toilets had long been emptied. The pub had belonged to an uncle of Jim and Regan's who had been willed it by its former owner. According to Regan, her uncle had for some time been the former owner's lover, an affair kept secret so as not to get either of them bashed up by the Mare's regulars, who suspected anyone who wore a pocket handkerchief or carried a newspaper – or worse, a book – to be a poof. The uncle, an accountant, had no idea how to run a pub, and had the grace to accept that he didn't have the charisma to carry off the role of publican. So he brought Jim in – Jim just back from Afghanistan with a bad hip – and died a year on. The former owner was commemorated by an unsmiling framed photograph behind the bar, beneath the spirits: moustachioed and beardless, the man had the soft, droopy eyes found in Flemish portraits.

When I arrived after three, the regulars were at their posts, starting in on the second and third pints of the day. A glassy-eyed man sat at the end of the bar, unspeaking, both elbows up, contemplating the pint resting between them. A builder with dirty knees and a high-vis jacket, pinching crisps from a packet unseamed on the table in front of him, looked over from time to time at the table where a big-breasted woman with a teased mound of cherry-coloured hair sat drinking a large glass of white wine and fiddling with her phone. Over the radio, the rugby.

'Look who's here,' said Jim when I came in. 'Look who's here.' He leaned across the counter, and I saw the place where his teeth had been knocked out and filled in on display. 'She's gone to pick up fags and milk,' he said. 'Shouldn't be long. What'll you have?'

'Half of Guinness,' I said.

'Christ,' he said with a grimace, and took my money. There was no pretence of my not paying. Jim's clientele, suffering from tarred lungs and cirrhosis, were leaking away to the undertaker's. His only hope was the trickle of customers who came in looking for a real local without televisions and pub quizzes and three-course Christmas dinners you signed up for in August.

'How's business?'

'Stamp duty gets paid,' he said. 'Just. And no one's come in today asking for a bloody cappuccino.'

The bell above the front door jingled and Regan walked in, dungareed like an artisan, and carrying a strained Tesco bag in each hand.

'All right, Margit,' she said, and handed the bags over the counter to Jim.

'What's this?' he said, and pulled out a carton of tofu.

'I'll have Staropramen,' she said, climbing on to a bar stool. 'Ta.'

'You bloody well won't,' he said, lowering the bags behind the bar. 'You owe me a shift.'

'I'll take my shift drink now, thanks, to keep my friend company. She's come all the way from Kilburn. All that way for a place that smells like feet.'

'I'm going to pretend I didn't hear that and see how Kev's doing at the end,' said Jim. 'Let you girls catch up.'

'I've tried to teach him,' said Regan to me. 'It's women, not girls, not birds – no blonde jokes, no jokes about hot flushes or periods – but the army's bent him. He's like a twelve-year-old.'

I asked whether any of Jim's army mates came to see him at the Mare.

'The few times I've met them,' she said, 'they seemed like a pretty quiet lot. They don't mind sitting around not saying anything. Jim won't see a soul about it, even when I tell him that everyone I know is in therapy. But then again they might just shut up because they know what I do and they don't trust anyone who's got a phone in one pocket and a pen in the other.'

'This place is Off The Record,' said Jim, overhearing Regan while coming over to pull Kev a pint of heavy-bottomed Foster's. 'I've told her. If I ever find out she's turned any of this or any of my customers into some rag or other, she's gone, she's not only off my couch, she's barred for good.'

'On the other hand,' Regan said, 'since you never set foot outside that door, I'd never see you again.'

'Ha bloody ha,' said Jim. 'Keep an eye on the till, will you. I'm going to see if that big bird with the phone needs another.'

'*Jim*,' said Regan. 'Shit. One day I'll be filing stories on his sexual harassment charges.'

I wouldn't have thought the red-haired woman was Jim's type – I'd always imagined him with, well, someone like his sister: short, scrappy, with a certain amount of mouth on her. But he lingered over the redhead's table, and she looked up, set down her phone, and began to run her hands through, or rather over, the headlands of her hair.

While Jim was away from the bar, Regan helped herself to a pint. As she waited for the froth of its head to settle, she told me she'd been spending the last few days looking at her notes from Harwich, teaching herself to read shipping manifests and bills of lading, and gathering crumbs of maritime law.

'It's a fucking free-for-all out there,' she said, and I could tell from her mixture of disgust and glee that it wouldn't be too long before she booked her passage on a container ship to Antwerp or Port Klang, the next instalment of the loose epic of her life. 'And you,' Regan said, hoisting herself onto a bar stool. 'Any leads on Lucan?'

'Very funny,' I said, and since she never took me seriously, not really, I told her I was looking into the missing forty-three. It was just as stupid a thing to say the second time as it had been the first, but it came out easier than before. Easier, I thought, and more convincing; even, perhaps, authoritative.

I was growing into it, I thought, the way you grow into a new title, the way a young actor grows into a theatrical role.

'You're looking into the what?' Regan said.

'The missing students,' I said. 'The Mexicans. I told you about them the other night.'

'How?' she said.

'What do you mean?' I said.

'How are you looking into them?' she said.

'I've been retracing their steps,' I said. 'You know: the way you do when you lose your money or keys. I've been following them. Like Sophie Calle.'

'Who the fuck is Sophie Calle?' she said.

I told her about the road from Tixtla to Iguala that I took yesterday, about the quarries at the side of the road, the foothills, about the way the scrub looks like fynbos. I had to explain fynbos: the bell-flowered mountainous shrubs which, as a child, I'd had to pick and paste into a book, carefully writing each common name, each scientific name, so many names the book couldn't close on them. The plants were too substantial, they didn't want to be in my book, they wanted to be back on the mountain. I told Regan about the odd pylon stretched in the distance, but it had been the vastness of the road that struck me, imagining it in the dark, with the mountains rising up around it. It made me think of Aztecs and their gods. Gods whose names were riddled with hieratic letters, letters crossed like bones or draped with the tailfeathers of impossible birds. The smoke that settled around the spines of the mountains was like the breath of those gods, and those mountainous spines like the vertebrae of dragons who lived thousands and thousands of years ago and were only sleeping until the great awakening broke their rest. The rocks of the mountains grew red, and only the occasional hitchhiker crouched warily against them. I saw roadworks where men sat in the meagre shade of a roadside tree; the occasional restaurant, its cloth awning stretched out, and some woman sprawled on a white plastic chair beneath the awning about to fan herself; and sometimes there were cacti and sometimes there were ferns and brightly coloured flowers of pink or orange or red so that I thought for a moment they were the signs of autumn, but no, the map said the footage had been taken in June 2014, only three months before those students took the same road to Iguala.

Regan looked like she wanted to speak, but I didn't seem to be able to stop myself, describing the odd labourer holding on to the back of a truck; the clouds coming in overhead and then blowing away; the burst tyre at the side of the road looped like a dead snake; the abandoned buildings, diggers teeth-deep in dust; the smoke winding along side roads. When the hills or gorges rose high on either side of me, I could see that what I had taken to be Mesoamerican hieroglyphs was graffiti painted on the grain of the rock. Outside a remote settlement, I saw a donkey tied to a tree and clothes hanging from a line. Once or twice I thought I saw white crosses at the side of the road, white as picked bone. At last, I crossed a wide copper-coloured river. How many crossings, how many roadworks, how many times could you be asked to stop by men with flags, and, before you knew it, get a gun or a knife thrust in your face?

Then Iguala was ten miles away, then seven miles, and even though the reports said several students fled into the hills during the attack, under sustained gunfire, the mountains still seemed far off, blue and stern, on the other side of

Iguala. It was all wrong, I told Regan. But I saw how many warehouses there were, or gated compounds, or houses behind high grey walls; and these buildings, which looked just as abandoned as the scrubland that led to them, seemed to be designed to hide people who would never be found. Places where, if you asked questions, questions you might have to underline with a certain force, no one could hear the answers. The odd truck driver with his window rolled down and his radio on might hear something that caused him to glance out of his window for a moment, before shrugging and driving on.

As I talked, Regan fiddled with her beer mat, bringing the end of her fingers sharply against its lip so that it vaulted into the air while she snatched at it with the same hand. 'Margit,' she said, laying down the beer mat after I finished. 'Is this some *Narcos* shit? Nat's working a hundred and fifty hours a week and you're at home watching Netflix? No offence,' she said, raising her hands, 'I'm not sure what this is.'

'It's an investigation,' I said. 'I'm trying to find out what happened.' It was the first time I had said it: the first full, open declaration of intent. I felt as if I had signed my name to a mortgage, and the thrill of possession was struck through with the terror of debt. 'Or at least,' I said, seeing her expression set into a mask-like impassiveness, as blank as one of Matisse's *masques*, 'I'm looking for a piece of what happened – the piece no one else is looking for.'

In the long pause that followed, I felt the space where moments before my lungs had worked ambitiously, expansively, bravely, now shrink. I could feel them straining against the hard walls of a locked cabinet.

'Far be it from me to tell you how to run your life,' Regan

said at last, 'but I'd be lying if I didn't say I had concerns. And there's basic protocol that you should remember,' she said, 'threshold procedures, professional standards.'

So there we sat: me and my low credit on one side, and on the other side, Regan with her portfolio of publications; Regan with her sources, her manifests and bills of lading. Regan with her ransacking, her pillaging, her razing, her burning of bridges, her laying waste to suburbs, her spoiling of the wells, her pollution of the lakes and lagoons, her rumour and plague, her poisoned arrows always finding their mark.

'I've got to go,' she said, looking at her phone. 'I'm meeting Wallis in forty-five minutes.' Wallis, I knew, was one of her editors. He went by his surname, since his given name was Quentin or Edmund and had been beaten out of him at school. 'You can come, if you like,' she said, as an afterthought. 'He'll behave if you're there.'

For a minute, I thought I'd walk out of the pub and never see her again. Then, when the minute passed, I understood that it was a problem of language. That, along with the missing forty-three, the words I needed to translate the investigation were missing too. This was the problem with the missing students, the reason that they had not been found: this silence they left behind, an inherited silence, a congenital silence. A silence born of complicity, of ultimatums and of unspeakable wagers: in short, every dialect of that language I had yet to learn.

17

Since Regan only had the one helmet, I waited for her to change into the leatherware and boots she called her suit before we took the Victoria line to Green Park, making our way from Piccadilly to the Red Lion in Crown Passage, where Wallis liked to drink. Going from the Mare to the Red Lion would make me laugh, she said, as we walked down St James's Street. Jim wouldn't have crossed the threshold even if he had a free pint waiting for him on the counter. But Wallis was an old queen, she said; he liked his boltholes; he liked to be a regular where he could wear his Magdalen scarf and know it would be recognized.

'I'm his bit of rough,' she said, as we rounded the corner on to King Street. 'He drags me out to hear how bad I've been.' When I asked if she was sure she wanted me with her, she told me I was her insurance.

The Red Lion might not have been licensed as a private club, but heads turned when we walked in. Quick, covert glances and unnecessary acts of chivalry pursued us across the floral carpet. At their tables, at the bar, men in venerably shabby tailored suits spoke in civil service whispers; in every corner, knowing handshakes, meaningful pauses, glances over the shoulder. Men with crinkled statesmen's faces, imperious noses and weak chins emptied their snifters of brandy. An atmosphere of veiled authority hung sleepily in the air that cigarette smoke had condensed a decade before, a benign but firm reinforcement of the way things were.

We found Wallis sitting at a table under a many-armed brass lamp, his chair positioned so that he could look up from his phone and peer over scholarly spectacles to observe who came in, who went out.

'It's been seven months since I've had a love letter from you, you bad girl,' he said to Regan as we sat down. He was a froggy man, round at the shoulders and the jaw: self-satisfied, his smile wide and lippy, his eyes small and unsurpriseable behind his spectacles.

'You didn't like the last one I sent,' she said.

'No,' he agreed, tilting his chin up to gaze through his bifocals, and then tucking his chin to his chest to look over the rims. 'Not quite up to your standard, I thought.'

Regan took this coolly. 'Did your drinks caddy come with you?' she said, looking around.

'Lamentably, even I must approach the bar,' Wallis said with an exaggerated pout, placing both signet-ringed hands on the table and heaving himself aloft. 'I shall perform my usual acts of divination.' He stood at the bar like a man without an umbrella waiting to hail a taxi in the rain, drenched but dignified. He returned with a glass of claret for himself, a pint of English ale for Regan, and a condescendingly sweet pear cider for me. I could imagine him in a tartan robe on a weekend, feet up, drinking tea and Alka-Seltzer, reading *How To Spend It* with a daub of Worcestershire sauce at the corners of his mouth.

'*Dites-moi,*' he said, when we'd settled in, 'what do the little birdies say?' When she didn't answer, he added, 'There must be a jingle. Give me the first few notes.'

'You know I don't talk about my projects until they're finished,' Regan said.

'What *can* she be living on?' he said with a touch of intrigue notionally thrown in my direction, but he was really only talking to his own gathered selves. For Wallis, I saw, I was playing Regan's legal counsel, ready to intervene at the first sight of blood, or her chauffeur, leaning with deceptive neutrality against the flank of her car. His career, I sensed, or perhaps it was his upbringing, had accustomed him to holding the stage around those with non-speaking roles.

He and Regan began to discuss people they knew in common: there was a vinegary anecdote about the BBC editor who'd picked up one of Regan's early stories, a lament for a fellow freelancer who'd finally taken a job at Wallis's paper but could no longer, as Wallis put it, get hard.

'It breaks my cold crust of a heart when I think about that man's sentences,' he said, and then asked Regan, 'Would it contravene your gospel to use an adjective?'

'Style is jism, Wallis,' she replied. 'That's why you like it.'

'You vulgar girl,' he scolded her. His extended index finger followed her up and down.

'Says the man who's been dressed by Jeeves,' she said.

'A literary reference!' said Wallis. 'I wasn't sure you could read.'

When we had finished our drinks, he looked at the platinum circle on his milky wrist. 'I've an idea,' he said.

18

We followed Wallis down Crown Passage past the younger men arriving to take their pint and cigarette – the editor casting regretful looks over his shoulder – and on to Pall Mall. 'My righteous brother is having a get-together at his club,' said Wallis as we walked. 'His wife's book has just been published (although *book* is a generous term from the pages I've seen), and I've promised to appear. I insist you come with me, as my shoulder pads, my Spanx. Help me hold my stomach in.'

Things happened when Regan was around, I'd always thought so. Until now, I'd never walked down Pall Mall, and here we were standing between the grand grey columns of the portico outside the Oxford and Cambridge Club with Toad of Toad Hall. There was a glint in Wallis's eye as he escorted us through the doors, Regan in her leather, me in what Nat called my librarian uniform: a cardigan, a pleated blue skirt that fell to the middle of my calves, and a pair of scuffed white plimsolls.

The manager, a stern man in his late thirties, assessed the quality of Regan's leather jacket and the length of her mini-skirt as he welcomed us. I was warmly but firmly invited to remove my cardigan; eyebrows ascended at the glimpse of my shoes. While the manager's attention was diverted, a woman in a grey sheath dress bent behind the meaty slab of marble which served as the club's front desk and furtively held out a pair of black pumps. She waited while I slipped into the alcove opposite and exchanged one pair of shoes for another, trying not to trip over the floor lamp. Through all of this, I expected Regan to vehemently object, to call on the shades of Wat Tyler and Gerrard Winstanley. Instead, she seemed amused as my discarded cardigan and plimsolls disappeared into a paper bag from Hobbs which the woman tactfully installed behind the desk. We walked on, as directed, through a maze of corridors, over patterned carpets, past sitting rooms impaled by titanic chandeliers at which Wallis shuddered. The pumps I had been given were a size too large and I was forced to slide my feet along the carpet as I walked, angling my feet upwards on the stairs.

'How,' hailed Wallis with a raised palm as we entered the North Library, a den of shelves, leather chairs, scholarly lamps and serious desks, where ten or so men and women in evening dress stood drinking. He kissed a red-haired woman on her freckled cheek. 'Well done, Mariam darling,' he said. 'Let's put it on the Booker longlist.' Beneath a copy of the Farnese Hercules, Wallis introduced Regan as his protégée and me – he paused – as . . .

'My assistant,' Regan offered.

'His brother is special projects editor at the *Guardian*,' she whispered in my ear as I watched Wallis and his brother shake hands. 'Wallis thinks he's a cunt because he pretends he hadn't been to Winchester and because he goes on about land redistribution at the family manor at Christmas.'

The brothers looked nothing alike – where one was round,

jovial, lewd, double-tongued, the other was grey, solemn, ascetic – except around their expressive mouths. Wallis's brother's mouth was tilted in disapproval, a habit which was the reason, I suspected, we had been invited: a younger brother's pleasure at pointing to the social hypocrisies of the elder – a liberal democrat who scowled at uninvited guests could not be trusted to maintain the moral line on immigration.

'Do help yourself,' Stewart Wallis said begrudgingly, gesturing to the table along the wall where empty glasses and uncorked bottles stood alongside propped copies of his wife's book, *The Sands of Time*.

According to the dust jacket, Mariam Renaudot's novel offered a lightly fictionalized account of her father's experiences in Algeria: the resignation of his commission, his conversion to Islam, his passionate but short-lived marriage to a tempestuous local woman, who I guessed was Renaudot's mother. The novel's title appeared in a calligraphic font against a stylized desert storm, but I had no reason not to toast the author when the first of the calls to raise a glass was given.

While Wallis introduced Regan to his sister-in-law, I had nothing to do but fiddle with the glasses and the books, the way amateur actors do when they don't know what to do with their hands. A professor of Abrahamic religions took pity on me, a beardless man with a weak chin and eyebrows electrified by exegesis. Mariam had consulted him as she wrote *The Sands of Time*, the professor told me in a confidential tone, and he had been delighted to offer his academic expertise. His own spiritual practice, he assured me, could be best described as humanistic in impulse, and he was disappointed to hear that I had been raised without what he called a 'divine story', since, I gathered, it was the subject on which he was most authoritative. By the time we escaped each other, I could see no sign of Regan. 'How would I know?' said Wallis, when I asked where she'd gone.

I left the library and discovered that the club was a carpeted Escher creation of stairs ascending and descending around each corner, of forked corridors leading up to suites or down to basement billiards and chaise longues; it echoed with the distant crack of rackets and the creak of the lift rising and falling in its ancient shaft; men in mustard trousers carried newspapers under arthritic elbows while wandering blindly past prints from *Punch*. When I was forced to cross paths with other occupants – the attendant in his creased waistcoat, the junior banker in his stout three-piece suit, the apple-cheeked American graduate student fresh from the squash court – I knew they could smell the red-brick on me, could sense that port gave me a headache, that I drank sherry only when Nat's father handed it round after church on Christmas Eve, and that I couldn't tell a court from a quad.

When at last I checked the terrace, I saw Regan in the far corner smoking with a woman I'd seen briefly in the library. The woman was tall, six feet tall at least, and wore a black jumpsuit under a men's red velvet dinner jacket. Her thick eyebrows, bony features and slash of a mouth gave her the look of a poet or a witch: not an English witch with hedgerow spells, but a real *bruja* who knew resurrection games and sex-magic. They were standing close together beside a fountain, and there was a secret charge to the way they faced each other. Regan was leaning back, elbows on the rail, shoulders open, while the other woman cupped the elbow of her smoking arm with her free hand. With the haggardness of the very thin, the tall woman levered her weight forward, an intention, a dare.

While I was still making up my mind about whether to interrupt them or to pack it in and go home, Regan saw me.

'Margit,' she called, and gestured for me to join her. 'This is Aurelia,' she said. 'Aurelia Olivera Cassou. God, what a name,' she said to her friend. 'It sounds like a typewriter.'

'Or a sneeze,' said her friend. From close up, I could see the gap between the tall woman's two front teeth, a slit between a pair of stage curtains.

She was one of Mariam's friends from Paris, she told me: a journalist, passing through London on her way home. As it happened, she and Regan knew each other, or rather they had met once before at a conference on new media in Amsterdam several years ago, which explained the electricity circuiting between them. For a while, Regan and Olivera Cassou, who was the sort of woman you could never imagine addressing by her first name, talked about the terrible weather in Amsterdam during the conference. No one had felt much like sleeping together because they were so depressed, a fact which was striking both in terms of conferences and in terms of journalists, Olivera Cassou said, and she should know. On the other hand, she said, looking around the terrace, British weather wasn't as bad as she'd been led to expect. The weather in Paris was much worse. 'When I first arrived in Paris, I was so cold,' she said. 'I wore tights every day and had a yeast infection for a year.'

Aurelia Olivera Cassou wore her hair around her ears, and the deep indentation between her eyebrows matched the hard red line of her mouth. When I asked her where she was travelling through London to, or, rather, where she had arrived in Paris from, she said she was originally from a small place in the north of Mexico called Santa Ana. 'Santa Ana *Viejo*,' she clarified, which was prettier and older than its sister. But as she'd been in Mexico City since she was seventeen, she could reasonably be called a Chilanga. Before I could add this to my map of tributaries – that is, before I could consider incorporating Olivera Cassou into my diagram of coincidences – I saw Regan glance at her phone and then slide it back into the pocket of her leather jacket. When she caught sight of me watching her, she reached into her other pocket for her cigarettes. There was something furtive in her movements, as if she was trying to pretend she hadn't been looking at the time, and I wondered if she'd placed a bet with herself – or with her friend – to see how long it would take me to extract this piece of information; if she had called me over in order to test how much of my training I'd retained.

'You're being modest,' Regan said easily as she lit her cigarette. 'Aurelia's a big deal in Mexico. A few years ago, she wrote a series of investigative pieces on a child-trafficking ring in Sonora that turned up a cache of local bigwigs.'

'Which is why I moved to Paris,' Olivera Cassou laughed. Her laugh was like the kind of circular saw that metal resists until, all at once, it gives way.

'That and the package *Le Monde* offered you,' Regan said.

'No comment,' said the other woman.

'So tell us,' said Regan, offering a cigarette first to me and then to her friend. 'How did you get it? The story on the trafficking ring.'

'This is where freelance gets you now, industry gossip?' said Olivera Cassou, dropping the fag end of her cigarette to smoulder on the terrace of the Oxford and Cambridge

Club, and reaching for another. 'If I die of cancer when I'm forty-five, I'll blame it on you, *comadre*.'

'Go on,' said Regan, but I knew this piece of theatre, this catechism, was meant for me.

'Shouldn't we try to find Wallis?' I said, but neither of them seemed to pay any attention.

'Let's see,' said Olivera Cassou, playfully bringing her hands together in a convent girl's pose, her cigarette sticking through her knuckles like a spiked signet ring. 'Ex-wives like to gossip, you know. They want a woman's sympathy. They want revenge on their fat husbands and their fat husbands' mistresses.' She raised her hands, palms up, an interceding saint. 'But seriously,' she said, and dropped her pose, sucked on her cigarette and exhaled in Regan's direction through loud pursed lips. 'I did what you do: credit cards, phone records. The odd policeman with a chip on his shoulder. But that was just luck, *comadre*: I just happened to be in the bar where a junior officer dropped by after being suspended. He'd lost evidence on the chief's orders and I was buying drinks. So,' she said, counting on her fingers: 'luck, human nature, alcohol. That's how babies are born.'

Olivera Cassou had finished her champagne and was drinking whiskey neat. Now's your chance, the look on Regan's face said. The problem is silence, I thought, and I remembered the way I had turned away from the Mexican embassy, its flag fluttering in exile, while the ambassador hid away at his desk, whispering intently into the phone.

'Did you follow Ayotzinapa?' I said at last, and I saw from the way she took the cigarette from her mouth, the quick rip and puckered breath, that Olivera Cassou was surprised. I also saw that she wasn't used to being surprised, or at least to this kind of surprise, the surprise of seeing two worlds fold over at the same corner.

'Did I follow Ayotzinapa?' Olivera Cassou repeated. 'God,' she said. 'I haven't heard anyone talk about Ayotzinapa for months.' It was the first time I'd heard someone say it out loud, *Ayotzinapa*, not heavy or sluggish the way it felt in my mouth, but like a bullet that curved upwards on its long trajectory and then dropped to the ground.

'Do you know anyone who worked on it?' I asked.

'We all worked on it,' she said, 'or we tried to. It was going to bring down the administration. It still might.' She seemed to be seeing me for the first time, or rather, examining me, the way an artist might look at a model before making the first mark on his blank sheet of paper. 'What do you know?' she said.

'I know a bit,' I said. 'The skeleton.' As soon as I'd spoken, I wished I'd chosen another metaphor.

'And who do you know?' she said.

'Who do I know?' I said.

'Yes, who are your contacts? Do you know Felix, Felix Vilar? Have you talked to Catulle Mendez? You can't work on the *normalistas* without running, stumbling really, into those two. Or Rosa Galba Orozco? Mexican journalists are so territorial: territorial and incestuous. These might seem like the same thing but they're totally different instincts, believe me.'

I wondered if Regan would jump in and give me away, but for the moment she seemed content to watch.

'I'm still mapping things out,' I said, cautiously.

'You have to talk to Catulle,' she said, 'though I'm sorry to say his English is terrible. Even when he lived in New York, he couldn't manage more than three words to a cab driver.

He told me he went around praying he'd run into a Puerto Rican. How's your Spanish?'

I would have prepared if I'd known I would be asked. Instead, the moment she spoke, I saw all the words I'd practised and transcribed, conjugated and memorized condense into one inky blot, a tick latched on to a spot on my scalp or behind my ear.

'*Non malo*,' I said at last, and the journalist frowned.

'Who do you work for?' she said.

'I'm on my own,' I said, and then, since this seemed like the wrong answer, I added, 'freelance.' At this, Olivera Cassou seemed to regain her distance, as if we were now sitting on separate sides of a pane of glass, and I saw I'd have to try another angle. 'Have you seen *Zodiac*?' I said.

'What?' said the journalist.

'It's a film,' I said, 'based on a true story. About the serial killer.' Never, I thought, had the words 'serial killer' sounded so stupid. 'It's in California. The Zodiac killer is killing couples, sending cryptic notes to the newspaper,' I said. 'The police are stuck, but one of the newspaper's reporters is on to it, and there's a cartoonist—'

'A cartoonist?' The hard red curtains of her mouth jerked at the corners.

'He works for the same newspaper as the reporter and he's really good at puzzles, so he decodes, or helps to decode, one of the serial killer's notes and gets brought on board – well, not so much brought on board as tolerated, sort of – and it goes on for years and the investigation goes nowhere—'

'Isn't it still unsolved, the Zodiac case?' said Regan, and I saw that her restlessness had been growing without my noticing it, and that she was ready to tamper with machinery.

'—the police drop it, the reporter is a drunk—' I continued, but it had been years since I'd seen the film and I was starting to doubt my memory of the plot.

'Now this sounds more like it,' said Olivera Cassou, and she drained her whiskey. She was, I guessed, a woman who drank but was never drunk: some caul, some spell kept her sober.

'So,' she said. 'You're the cartoonist?'

'I could be the cartoonist,' I said. 'I could be *a* cartoonist.'

'You think you'll find what we couldn't,' she said.

Careful, I thought.

'Listen,' she said, tossing back her whiskey and setting down the glass. 'What you want to do isn't just insulting, it's impossible. It's like a kid from Chiapas who decides he'll prove that the royal family killed Princess Diana. Only he doesn't know anything about the paparazzi, he doesn't even know where Buckingham Palace is. His English is worse than my friend Catulle's, so he can't read the newspapers, even if he could afford them. He's just seen the pictures of the crash and he's watched the interviews and the funeral and his heart bleeds, not for Diana, you know, not for women forced into marriages they don't want, or controlled by institutions, or treated as whores, but for his own shitty life in Chiapas where he has to borrow his cousin's motorbike to work seven days a week at a plastics factory, or lay cement, to support his girlfriend who is pregnant with a baby she says isn't his.'

As she talked, I saw that the Mexican woman's extravagant teeth were the most witch-like thing about her: oracular, devious, pointed and angling for space.

'Let me tell you,' she continued. 'My friend Jorge, Jorge who wrote the best fucking copy – anyone who ever edited him swore it. He wrote plays in his spare time – they were never staged, naturally, but Jorge could catch the way life is sometimes like a play. But this theatre doesn't let you out between the acts, my friend, you'll learn this soon if you haven't by now, and he stuck his neck out, didn't take the money, once, twice, and didn't move away like a coward, not even when we told him he was being stupid, more than stupid, reckless, and then—'

She exhaled with a pop, dropped her cigarette, and ground out its sparks with her toe as if it were a spider she'd found in the corner of her bedroom.

'Once his body was flown back to Mexico City, his mother was so furious that she stopped all his friends, all of us, his editors and colleagues, from coming to the funeral, she even burned the cards and left the flowers outside her house to rot, because she wanted nothing to do with the people who let him go on with his work, who told him how good he was, who praised his bravery even while they told him to take precautions, keep a low profile, stay at home, or better yet, leave Veracruz, leave the country for a while, take up the fellowship in Canada, take the job at *Le Monde*. I wasn't their first choice, you know,' she said to Regan.

'What I mean is,' she said, turning back to me, 'you can't use analogies. If you want to use analogies, go into another line of work. Write novels, like Mariam. I've thought about it myself, you know,' she said to Regan. 'Writing a novel. How hard can it be? I'll join a writers' group in the troisième arrondissement where everyone drinks wine and says nice things about each other's manuscripts. But if I did,' she said to me, 'I'd be really fucking sure where the line was.'

I wasn't sure which line she meant – whether it was the line between analogy and fact, or between one analogy and another, or the line between fiction and real life, or between the things you know and the things you can only speculate on, or even the things that get you promoted and the things that get you shot – but I didn't ask. I could see from the look in her eye that I'd run out of questions. I left the two of them on the terrace of the club not long after to finish whatever business they'd started in Amsterdam, or to mock my Spanish behind my back, or to start referring to me, between themselves, as *the cartoonist*, in the small cruel way of new lovers, a nickname I couldn't object to, not really, since I'd handed it to them on a platter.

19

Just like that, the summer died and Halloween was on the horizon, copies of Francis Ford Coppola's *Dracula* cropping up on special offer at Sainsbury's. On Twitter, I saw that Helen had published a paper on Iosi Havilio in a Spanish-language literary journal based in Leeds, and that the Farbers were taking *Figura* back to Chicago. The magazine's feature this month was on a kind of art called seminal pop and contained a heated discussion over whether female artists could or couldn't make it.

For a few days after my visit to the Oxford and Cambridge Club, I had nothing to do with the missing Mexicans. It was like a hangover, the kind that sours a favourite drink. I closed all the tabs, shelved Bolaño, put my notebook in a drawer, and still a queasy taste in my mouth, the spongy bruise on my chest, lingered on. Like a hangover, all the stupid phrases I'd come out with at the club and on the terrace stayed with me all day. The missing students had been a kind of drunkenness, a glowing coherence that was mangled whenever I tried to put it into words. Now the elation had passed, and there was only a headache, bloating, an unsettled stomach.

Long ago, before he and Helen had broken up, Alex told

me about the time he was mugged in Rome. He had deserved it, he said. He had drunk too much vodka at a club in a warehouse on the outskirts of the city and because the air was finally cool and the moon was full, he had decided to walk back to his hotel. There had been three or four of them, he thought, but at times during what followed it had felt like there were six of them, seven, even eight – each of them a limb of some kind of rabid animal. The thieves took everything he had on him and beat him up for good measure. He couldn't remember how he'd got back to the hotel, he said, but he did. After the mugging, he said, he slept for days. He got out of the bed to piss and every now and then to phone the front desk for something to eat. Otherwise, he lay there, swimming in and out of sleep. When he woke up, his arms and legs didn't feel like they belonged to his body, they felt like they had been chopped off and stacked on top of each other. Sleep happened to him, he said. It jumped on him as suddenly as the boys who had left him in this condition.

In the days after my meeting with Aurelia Olivera Cassou, I too slept more than usual, and my sleep was catastrophic, brutal. Nat asked if I was coming down with a virus, but I wondered if I was getting rid of one, if Regan's friend had been a kind of doctor or apothecary who, with her experience and her moral high ground and her disinterest, had tried to purge me of it. Would it have been too much to ask for an introduction to one of the friends she had mentioned in passing? One of those territorial and incestuous journalists, Felix Vilar, or even Catulle Mendez, with his terrible English, or the mysterious Rosa Galba Orozco? Would it have cost her so much to scribble down a phone number or even an email address on a scrap of whatever paper she had to hand?

After a few days of uneasy recovery, the nausea was less acute and I felt able to go over our conversation again. I wrote down as much of it as I could, the way sad-eyed Johannes once said you should suck poison out of a snakebite. I tried to look at the Mexican's critiques objectively: the question of language, and contacts, and sources, and moral seriousness, which is what I understood the point of the story of her friend Jorge to have been.

And then there was the fact of the package which arrived a few days after she'd dismissed me. The package arrived with no sign of its sender, no return address or note, but only one person could have sent me copies of Elena Poniatowska's *La noche de Tlatelolco*, Anabel Hernández's *La verdadera: noche de Iguala*, Sergio González Rodríguez's *Los 43 de Iguala*, and a Spanish-to-English dictionary. I understood immediately what it meant: that Olivera Cassou would not introduce me to Vilar, Mendez or Orozco – she could not, would not do my work for me – but she would give me another chance to prove myself worthy of my own self-respect. Out came the notebook and the novels of Bolaño, which were pulled off the shelf and put back on the bedside table. Not that they were useful for any part of the investigation, not that they were proof of anything; they were amulets, not even Aurelia Olivera Cassou could begrudge me that. How is a book so different from a crucifix? Everyone knows Sontag went around Vietnam with a sacred ring she never wore but kept in her pocket; even Carl Bernstein had a lucky brand of cigarettes.

20

Twenty-one kilometres from Iguala along México 51 lies Cocula, a dusty outback town with several finely painted buildings behind high gates. The town's police station failed to appear on the map. The Iguala police station, according to Google Maps, had also closed. In May 2009, according to Street View (five years and four months before the night in question), the San Juan River in Cocula was so dry a cow could stand on the gravel bottom and find no water to drink. Further along the river, in a town called Apipilulco, the still water was the colour of a dead frog. But it was where the river crossed Cocula, the San Juan River, that black refuse bags containing material matching the remains of one of the students from Ayotzinapa, Alexander Mora Venancio, were found at the end of October 2014, and identified in early December by forensic specialists brought in from the University of Innsbruck. The discovery of the remains of Alexander Mora Venancio, said the government, was proof, evidence of the Historical Truth. Anyone could see that a confederacy of crooked local cops had handed the students over to Guerreros Unidos to shoot or strangle and then burn them. If motivations were thin on the ground, you could always depend on the inexplicable nature of evil.

The black bags were a convincing touch. Unwanted things are always dropped or pitched or shovelled into refuse sacks, although it's true that once, outside a corner shop, I saw a grizzled skeleton of a man place an apple tenderly inside a black bag he was wearing like a glove on his other hand. He was a street artist, a collector. For everyone else, a black bag means contamination, leakage and stink: shorthand for dissolving weeds or spoiled food, things in states between solid and liquid, soured yogurt, mouldy soup, things no one wants put in the ground, at least not their ground. A convincing touch, this piece of stagecraft, the remains of Alexander Mora Venancio discovered in a black bag in the San Juan River near Cocula. An admission, too, perhaps, of the inconvenience and wastefulness of the whole business, the enormous expenditure of government energy in keeping this show on the road.

There are those who believe like Walter Benjamin that a work of art has a certain aura, that they can tell a Vermeer from a van Meegeren, or a Picasso from something by Elmyr de Hory. It's not a question of brushstrokes, they'd say. You can't make a masterpiece, as the forger Eric Hebborn suggested you could, by getting a little drunk and carrying the line. It's a comprehensiveness of mind, a sense of vision. There might not have been a presiding genius on the night of 26 September either: all signs pointed, in fact, to the absence of it, to some constellation of instinct, harnessed momentarily and then let loose. The government had to sketch the events, to crosshatch them, to deepen the perspective, to forge coherence. I was beginning to think that this narrative, this Historical Truth, was itself a forgery, like the recent Modigliani exhibition in Genoa: one act in the style of another, with false provenance, spoiled archives, amended paper trails and borrowed signatures. A few facts given, a story given just enough substantiating detail to convince the buyer who considered himself a man of good taste. The price was right – he was thinking long term. It satisfied him for the moment; when he was tired of it, he'd sell. Meanwhile, it solved the problem of the blank wall.

21

My neighbour's sons had been digging a firepit at the end of their garden, and it was only a matter of time before one boy pushed the other in. The ceremony would generally begin around five when there was some question of a barbecue, though I could see from the window above the sink the unused barbecue set bought last year for a wet August bank holiday. The fire always took a while to coax into being. Then one boy would put a log onto the pit in excitement and dampen the young blaze. The other would put the whole packet of firelighters into the pit when his father was turned the other way. One evening, the older boy laid an entire weekend spread on the fire. As the fire caught, the pages lined themselves in electric orange. I watched as the heat ruffled the paper, so that the supplements began to ripple and preen like a book of spells. When the newspaper launched itself from the flames, it rose into the air, a terrifying apparition tearing itself apart at its fringes. The boys stared as it flaked apart, moving on the air like a burning balloon. The flaming spirit they'd raised threatened to drift into another garden, to brush against the roof of the wooden shed, to scorch a table or a sheet left out to dry, but in the end there was no need to call the emergency services. The paper went out, just like that, and dropped, exhausted, a vanished apparition.

On most fire nights, my neighbour's wife came out with her glass of wine, leaned against the doorjamb and watched the festival of flame. The only time I liked her was when she was looking at the fire her boys built: only then did I ever see she could stare at something and be silent.

'They're going to see you one day,' said Nat, 'and they're going to call the police.'

What could I say? One life is not enough. I need several, packed together, to make up the sum.

22

When I worked on my Spanish, I thought of the Delphic cavern of Aurelia Olivera Cassou's mouth, the escarpment of her teeth around which that stream of language navigated as it crossed her tongue. I memorized *cinturón*, belt, *cuchillos*, knives. I learned that a *maestro* was not a conductor but a teacher; *conductor* not a conductor but a driver; *empresario* not a manager of a theatre or an opera house but a businessman. It was a language of false friends and smuggled differences, and each rope bridge I built was quickly cut loose: *espejo* a mirror not a species, *cartera* a wallet not a map. Nat said nothing about the dictionary that had appeared overnight, or the scraps of paper on which I practised my conjugations. Spanish was the bastard child he was determined to overlook. He was biding his time as I raised it, waiting to see how much of me would come to show in its face.

Meanwhile, from the coffee table, the books which had arrived in the anonymous package smirked, holding who knew how many hints, leads and answers. The author of *Los 43 de Iguala* was no longer living, I learned when I looked up Sergio González Rodríguez: the result not of a narco's bullet, his obituaries stressed, but of ordinary causes, a heart attack at the age of sixty-seven. But in another sense, in a truer sense, he would live for ever, not only because of his own books, which seemed to be numerous and untranslated, an extensive bibliography which included several novels as well as the work of non-fiction on my coffee table, but also because – out of friendship and artistic licence and perhaps not a little mischief – his friend Roberto Bolaño had put him in *2666*, an act of affectionate vandalism, or perhaps a cut-and-paste job, the way you replace the faces in famous paintings with the faces of your friends, roughly scalped from photographs of them you find on Facebook. It took me nearly half an hour to find the place where González Rodríguez appeared in *2666* (why don't novels have indexes?), but I found him at last.

> Sergio González was thirty-five and recently divorced, and he was looking to make money anywhere he could. Normally he wouldn't have accepted the assignment, because he was an arts writer, not a crime reporter. He wrote reviews of philosophy books that no one read, not the books or the reviews, and sometimes he wrote about art shows or music.

The character Bolaño made from his friend – the character he cast, you could say, as one copies a classical sculpture to admire and study its sculptor's technique – was always referred to as Sergio González, never by his full name, Sergio González Rodríguez. This omission or amputation of one of his names seemed to turn the remaining names into a kind of nickname or shorthand, underlining the fact that the character was a shadow, a double, of the living counterpart, and that their correspondence was like the unknowable and slightly sinister relationship between the doubles in certain portraits by Frida Kahlo, which shared the same bloody network of veins and arteries. I wondered if González Rodríguez had minded being cast into his friend's novel, if he'd minded the shabbiness of his debut: disappointed in love, short of money, dabbling at writing in various genres, sleeping with whores, an amateur in every sense of the word. Or if he'd thought, fuck it, I'm going to be kind of famous. Had Bolaño kept it a secret until the last minute, until the book was in the windows of every good Spanish bookshop the world over, and he was dead and buried? Or had he made up some sort of Villa Diodati wager, whereby the first one to convincingly sneak the other into a novel would take home his first edition of *Moby-Dick*? But you already have it, González Rodríguez might have pointed out, and Bolaño might then have confessed that, given the precarious state of his finances, he was considering selling it through a local antiquarian bookdealer. Now, both tenants of whatever afterworld they had moved on to, they could challenge each other to perform feats of memory, poetic and mathematical, to pass the time.

The first sentence of González Rodríguez's book read: *He querido evitarlo, pero me resulta imposible.* Since I understood neither *He* nor *querido* nor *evitarlo*, the distance between us seemed greater than ever. When the postcard-sized English translation of González Rodríguez's book arrived in the mail, I saw that I needed a dictionary more than ever. The Mexican writer was partial to words like 'tellurian' and 'ultra-capitalism', slipping in phrases like 'technified barbarism', 'institutional formalism', the 'pro-persona principle' and 'anti-institutional synergy'. He threw around 'negative emanations', the 'politics of barbarism' and 'intrahistory'. I had no idea what 'geostrategic phenomena' were, or what 'convergent impunity' or 'cosmovision' was. I imagined him, at two or three in the morning, after a raucous night had burned back to its embers but before the sadness set in, smoking cigarette after cigarette, smelling of sweat and whiskey, proudly recalling his youthful anti-authoritarianism. In his heart, González Rodríguez still thought of himself as the musician he had been when he had played in his brother's band, whose album *Enigma!* was named as one of the twenty-five best Iberoamerican rock albums of the 1970s by *Rolling Stone*, a fact he did not omit from his account of the missing students of Ayotzinapa. Maybe it was this artistic past, to which his friend Bolaño's novel mischievously alluded, that encouraged his inclination for dramatic phrases. 'Before I go to sleep each night,' he wrote,

> a deep murmur reaches my ears that tends to reach the point of desperation. In that instant, as my anguish borders on a sudden vertigo, I'm able to perceive that the sound comes from some subtle point, remote and internal, beneath the everyday . . .

His desk, he wrote, was a proliferating archive of its own, covered with documents, reports, photographs, recordings. I pictured him sitting soberly, or maybe not so soberly, among the objects of his kingdom, a detective in a dark room lit only by the grizzled end of a cigarette, with a bottle open on his desk and a hat cocked on the ear of his chair. Like all detectives, he had a weakness for doomed women. In his cups, he was guilty of pontificating, true, but perhaps such events demanded such a tone. At other times, he sounded like a political candidate, an underdog making manifestos to carve into stone. Nothing in these pages is fiction, he wrote, but sometimes he made it sound like it. In the strangest part of his book, González Rodríguez described arriving at a literary festival in Bilbao, losing a suitcase, missing a taxi, and finding his hotel by chance. He could barely sleep that first night in Bilbao, he wrote, a problem which spilled over from the time he had spent in Germany just before disembarking in Spain. The hotel he had stayed at in Berlin the week before was near the Hauptbahnhof and a power station, and he had slept poorly for the four or five nights he was in that northern city, a fact which he attributed to his sensitivity to disturbances of any kind. Now, upon eating breakfast in Bilbao (a café con leche, perhaps, alongside a sweet roll with a dollop of jam, globules of which clung to the coarse hairs of his sparse moustache), he discovered the origin of the previous night's sleeplessness. As improbable as it sounded, the origin of his discomfort was Frank Gehry's Guggenheim, which stood across the street, the prime position of his hotel suggesting, I thought, that the peso was not so weak a currency, nor the position of Mexican journalists so modest, as some had claimed. 'In a hallway on the third floor,' he wrote,

I located the heart of the museum: a point at which the entire structure of the building seemed to tremble under my feet. The sensation was shocking, electromagnetic, savage: it was as if I had come in contact with the building's sacred spot. I quickly fled, my pulse racing, frightened by the certainty that I could have destroyed the building with a precise blow to this spot, its invisible fulcrum. I had intuited and observed the secret of the museum, the intersection that revealed its energy.

I copied this paragraph down in my notebook, although it seemed to have no obvious connection to the missing students. Or rather, I copied it because its connection was structural, even architectural, rather than substantive. More than anyone, I thought, he would have understood the diagrams I had drawn. In fact, this paragraph of González Rodríguez's seemed to describe my diagram of coincidence, even though it was a description written without him ever having seen the image it translated. Nonetheless, the image of the author stunned and then startled into escape was undeniably ridiculous, as if he were a rabbit who'd dashed into the highway in the middle of the night, only to see the bright beams of trucks bearing down on him, but it was a ridiculousness he didn't hide or cringe from, a ridiculousness which, paradoxically, he took seriously, and declared in print for all to see.

I copied too the facts he offered as evidence of a cover-up. That Cocula, where the ashes of Alexander Mora Venancio were discovered in contentious – not to say disputed – circumstances, meant 'place of quarrels' in Nahuatl. That leftist teachers and guerrillas occasionally joined forces with organized crime to disrupt the corrupt and incompetent local government. That in 2011, three years before the disappearances, students had held a protest in Chilpancingo by blocking the highway, and two students had died following a subsequent clash with the police, along with a man who succumbed to his injuries after the students tried to burn down the garage where he worked. I learned that, just as human traffickers were called *coyotes*, the spies sent out by organized crime were known as *falcons*. That organized crime controlled the country's iron exports to China. That

the large-scale cultivation of marijuana and opium was introduced into Guerrero by a CIA operative; that CIA agents had
been recorded as being present on that fateful night in Iguala;
and that the mutilation and eye-gouging of Julio César
Mondragón Fontes that took place north of the Periférico
Norte on the night of 26 September resembled certain covert
protocols deployed in Vietnam. Most provocatively, González
Rodríguez argued that there had been at least one soldier on
active duty who had infiltrated the students' circle and who
had died among them: the deceptively quiescent Julio César
López Patolzin, who, on the government's poster, it was true,
looked a good fifteen years older than the others.

The trial of the members of Guerreros Unidos who had
been hauled up before a judge, González Rodríguez maintained, was a sham. The words of the prosecutor, Attorney
General Jesús Murillo Karam, were stirring: he was prosecutor as witness, prosecutor as chief mourner. And yet, while
the government's circumstantial evidence rested on the two
black bags of ashes found at Cocula which allegedly included
the remains of Alexander Mora Venancio, a researcher at the
Physics Institute of the National Autonomous University
of Mexico (UNAM) calculated that the cremation of all
forty-three students at the Cocula rubbish dump would have
required '33 tons of firewood or 995 tyres, which would have
left behind 2.5 tons of steel wire', which, needless to say, was
not discovered at the site. Be that as it may, the National
Human Rights Commission, an ostensibly independent body
given an A rating by the Global Alliance of National Human
Rights Institutions, corroborated the government's Historical
Truth and affirmed the Cocula rubbish dump as the site of
the crime, the final resting place of the missing forty-three.

Meanwhile, Captain José Martínez Crespo, a commander in Chilpancingo who was responsible for the infantry battalion whose base was two miles away from the scenes of the crimes it was responsible for cordoning off on the streets of Iguala, and who later refused permission for an official inspection of that base to take place, was subsequently promoted. I learned that the name Iguala comes from the Nahuatl for 'where the night settles down'.

By the time I was through with González Rodríguez, once I'd read him through twice from start to finish, *The Iguala 43* looked like a teenager's copy of *Wuthering Heights*: marked, question-marked, exclaimed, underlined, starred and bracketed. I leaned over the side of the bath and set the book down on the dry mat, then sat back to watch the condensation bead and trickle down the white tiles and over the geometric clusters of blue and green that interrupted the blank surface. 'I have learned,' wrote González Rodríguez, 'that investigation is a job where one needs to trust in one's self.' As long as I was in the bath, I couldn't grasp the size of my own body, or how the parts above the water related to the parts below. Everything submerged seemed to belong to someone else, to a dead woman lying on a coroner's table. 'I will venture a definition that has been useful, at least for me, in guiding my work,' wrote González Rodríguez: 'investigating events is an art of rationality, logic, criticism, intuition, practicality, experimentation and openness.' I tried to put Sergio González Rodríguez's words into Nat's mouth, but it was like putting a mask on a mannequin, or covering his face with a home-made balaclava, a pair, say, of women's tights. All it did was make me see that he would never say them. Then I leaned back in the tub and imagined I was in the passenger seat of a car, an old car, a Datsun. In the picture in my mind, it was dusk or just before and the windows were rolled down so that my hair kept blowing into my mouth. Sergio González Rodríguez was at the wheel wearing a pair of cheap sunglasses to keep off the sun. We said nothing, all we were doing was driving. We drove towards the horizon, towards clarity, and they were one and the same thing.

23

A thousand years ago, when we were still struggling with the pathetic fallacy, we chanted Tennyson to Mrs Lurie in a classroom near the cricket pitch. *Willows whiten, aspens shiver. / The sunbeam showers break and quiver* . . . We didn't know what aspens were, or bearded barley, all we knew were aloes and pepper trees, but all of us, even the van Rensburg twins, who told jokes their father had made about Nelson Mandela's penis (jokes Nina said I must on no account repeat), liked the words that shunted back and forth like one of the looms the local craft museum took out once a year to remind us of our old artisanal ways. She'd been an early adopter, the Lady of Shalott, weaving her web, her mirror, that technology which let her see without being seen. She was like Sophie Calle with her wigs and her right-angled lens.

Had I been too square in my methodology? Had I kept my hands too clean and wiped the soles of my shoes on the carpet in front of every threshold I crossed? I had neither partner nor assistant; my investigation was free from handbooks and regulations, from paperwork and justification of taxpayer expense. In fact, you could say it was González Rodríguez who signed off on my request: González Rodríguez, who I was already thinking of as a kind of commanding officer, or detective inspector, a godfather in the way that Bolaño could never have been a godfather: he was always the uncle who showed up once a year, drank too much or stayed sober, and disappeared in the middle of the festivities. It was González Rodríguez, after all, who believed investigation should be experimental and intuitive as much as it was rational and practical, so you could say it was because of González Rodríguez that I found Mother Pacifica.

24

There was a smell of old laundry about the business of talking to the dead, an aroma of sadness staining ancestral curtains and family quilts. It was an industry of flattened women storing up affection in their collections of ceramic shepherd boys and commemorative spoons so disheartening that I nearly changed my mind and went to the tarot reader on Blackburn Road instead.

The address on Mother Pacifica's website took me to a chalky Victorian building on Kilburn High Road which once belonged to a firm of solicitors, and the painted ghost of their names, Connolly and Whyte, still clung to the flaking front between crumbling pediments and garlands of plaster. The pavement in front of the building was lined with mothers in billowing black pushing their young past betting shops, nail salons, sellers of wigs and weaves, discounted plastic washtubs, baskets of towels and Jaffa Cakes, trays of wholesale fruit and vegetables, shops that sold phone cards and wired money abroad. A few rumpled, scowling white women with their orange hair scraped back from their foreheads paced up and down, fags in hands. Older men in white gowns and kufis drank coffee at tables on the pavement, serenely watching the parade.

Inside Mother Pacifica's building, two sharp flights of stairs carpeted in dusty crimson led on to a compressed landing. A pair of letting agents dressed in navy suits and bearing impressively monogrammed folders squeezed past, leaving a sharp smell of hairspray and perfume samples behind them. No incense lingered around number 6, no third eye on the door. I expected my knock to be answered by a middle-aged woman with dark curls streaked with white at the temple, an imposing nose and a pair of harem trousers; or by a witch in a loose kimono and turban, trailing cockerel feathers and dried leaves. To my surprise, the door was answered by a lean brown boy, full-grown but slight. He stood in the doorway with a sense of vagueness, a borrowed responsibility, a preference for somewhere else.

'I'm looking for Mother Pacifica,' I said.

'You've found her,' the boy said. He had a wide forehead, made wider by his blank expression. In his stiff blue jeans and grey sweatshirt, he had the look of someone who was lean by intention rather than nature. Some memory of deprivation stuck to him, his slack way of standing in the door. He could be a thief, I thought; even now, on the other side of the door held open so slackly, so carelessly, the boy's partner might be putting Mother Pacifica's money into a holdall.

'I've found her,' I repeated, uncertainly.

He let the door swing fully open and turned away, expecting me to follow him. 'I found the name in a magazine,' he said. 'I liked it. It made me think of the ocean.'

I half expected him to tell me he saw me coming.

'I thought—' I said, as I stepped into a large room

furnished with several well-worn couches placed at talkative angles. The room was south-facing and bathed in shallow light, its only plant life a clutch of paper roses wilting in a vase. Outside, on the window ledges, pigeons flirted and bickered. The walls were bare except for the aquariums: two set on top of each other and crowded with what looked at this distance like fireflies. It was an odd room, a carpeted studio with a barebones gallery kitchen opposite the aquariums: a small fridge, a sink, a kettle. It was impossible to imagine someone living here, impossible to make it cohere, to draw its objects together for a purpose. I couldn't shake the feeling of impersonation: the conviction that he'd never been in this room before, that he had happened to find himself here, and me at the door, and that he had accepted it without a fight.

He closed the door and sat on a musty floral couch, crossing his legs beneath him. 'Do you smoke?' he asked, as I took my seat opposite him on a kinked rust-coloured love seat. I felt he ought to know the answer already.

'I quit two days ago,' he said, 'and I wouldn't have said no to temptation. You think about it all the time. It blocks up the wires.' He put his hands together in his lap and gave a small sigh. 'What can I do for you?' he said. 'Love trouble?' He expected it to be a man I'd met, some man on a train or at a bar, I thought, or a dead father: the pattern of female curiosity he knew best.

'I want to find someone,' I said, 'a group of someones. I want to know if they've—'

'Crossed over,' he offered.

'Passed,' I said. As soon as I said it, I saw I'd given myself away as a coward.

'You don't know if they've passed?' he said.

'Is that a problem?' I said.

'Well,' he said, making a face, his chin jutting forward in punctuation, marking the spot where I should take note, 'it's a bit like fishing in a lake that might have no fish—' (I make no promises, he was saying, you understand) '—But no, it's not a problem.' For a moment, I thought I saw a bristle of professional pride come over him, and then I understood that trafficking with the dead was as competitive as any other business. 'Tell me about them,' he said, 'the people you're looking for.'

But I didn't know how to tell just one part of the story: it ran like a window crack, in all directions. I started with the buses on their way north, the snarl of the roads, the peripheries and the crossroads, the rain and the gunfire and the night, but one thing led to another, and the night reminded me of the photograph of those girls waiting under their tarp, and then I thought of the women of Troy in the painting by Christoforo Reyes, and the mothers waiting at home for their sons, as well as the people who ran for the hills, and the others who were found buried in those hills, the ones no one was looking for, not to mention those who got lost in the desert, those who crossed more borders than they were expecting. It was like a labyrinth, this story, each thread branching off and coiling in on itself, and then splitting, or even bifurcating, like Regan's tattoo, and maybe Joanna's friend the philosopher was right, maybe contingency with its branching roots is more important than coincidence after all. I trailed off, each clause growing quieter and more tentative, and waited for Mother Pacifica to respond. He didn't, not right away. He'd asked for a sketch, after all, and I'd handed him a Hieronymus Bosch, something with too many mouths, too many legs, too many objects out of their elements, too many disturbances, too many incongruities, too many tails, horns and slits, too many reversals and inversions, too much out of sequence, beyond causality, something altogether too perverse or too exhausting.

'Fuck it,' Mother Pacifica said at last, and reached beneath one of the cushions he was sitting on for a pack of cigarettes. 'Do you have anything that belongs to them?' he said, rummaging in the couch's side cavities and intercostal muscles for a lighter.

I was prepared for this. I'd brought a copy of the government poster with the photographs of the missing students that I'd downloaded and printed at a stationer's on the High Road. 'This is it?' he said doubtfully, looking down at the badly pixelated photographs, those thumb-sized smudges of identity. I'd also brought my diagrams and notebooks with me, along with several of Bolaño's novels and the cheap jewellery box with the word MEXICO in artificial mother-of-pearl on its lid, but they were for me, these relics, they were not for show. If I laid them out in the open, I was afraid they'd shrink or bleach.

Mother Pacifica ran a hand over his face. He whet his knuckles along his jaw, stood up, walked to the windowsill and extinguished his cigarette in a mug with 'University of Southampton' printed on it, while I waited like a poor inventor hawking my patent. When he sat down again, the sense of impersonation that had been hanging over him was gone.

'All right,' he said. 'Think of it as like tapping a phone.' From the new smoothness in his voice, I could tell it was a well-oiled metaphor. 'Like an old phone operator with a switchboard. I'm going to drop in on several lines and see what I can pick up. You'll have to be patient,' he warned me. 'Sometimes they babble, sometimes they've got nothing to say. They have lapses, same as us.'

When he closed his eyes, I wondered if he was going to speak in a different voice, a deeper voice, but he was quiet. The quiet stretched on for so long I began to feel alone. It was like the first time you sleep with someone and they fall asleep, forgetting or letting go, when they are unconscious, of whatever they might say or do; and you can't sleep at all because you are too excited, or because you are afraid of what might happen if you lose control of yourself; and the person lying next to you continues to sleep, unreachable and remote, and there is nothing you can do to join them, you can only acknowledge the infinite separation between people, the impenetrable solitude of your skulls.

Then Mother Pacifica said, 'Come out.'

Shouldn't he speak more softly? I wondered. Surely manners are more important to the dead than to the living: all they have left is form. (They might not be dead, I told myself, they might be in some border factory, or in a private army. They might be drug-running. They might be reciting Marx or Hugo around a campfire. They might be digging other people's graves.)

'There you are,' he said, or rather whispered, the way you might talk to a wild animal with nails or teeth it would use if startled. 'I'm listening,' he said.

But what could he hear? I'd never thought of heaven as a great shore, or a long street, or a rustling wheat field. It occurred to me now that the afterlife might be a hard country, a rugged terrain with few places to hide from the sun in the day, or the sharpness of the air at night; a country rich in scrubland and shadow and stars and night-blooming flowers, and an unevenness to the ground that made you look where you were going. You could see each other coming from a mile away. Not much congregation, not much talk.

Through the floorboards above us, feet trod and shuffled. They passed over our heads from room to room, getting thicker and heavier, as if all the souls we were looking for were above us, crowded and scuffling, trying to get our attention. But Mother Pacifica was deaf to them and me both. His arms had stiffened and his forehead creased with concentration. Like it was on the tip of the tongue but just out of reach: like you had to move towards it, make yourself ready for it, spread your legs a little wider so the crest came towards you, unhurrying, undistracted, until you were in the rip tide. Then his eyes opened. 'You didn't think it'd be that easy, did you?' Mother Pacifica said, and his face cracked into a smile.

25

Thank you for your interest, said my inbox. Thank you for your recent application. We regret to inform you. We're sorry to announce. I am sorry to inform you. Unfortunately. The record number of applicants. The high volume of applicants. The high quality of the high volume of the record number of applicants. We wish you all the best. We thank you for your interest. We wish you every success in your future endeavours.

26

Later that afternoon, walking in soggy circles around Queen's Park to tire myself out, I saw how stupidly I'd gone about the whole business. At least, I saw that I'd fallen at the first hurdle, that I should have found a medium who spoke Spanish. I should have asked her to call up Julio César Mondragón Fontes or Alexander Mora Venancio, the ones who were, without a doubt, beyond. Having an insider among the shadows – a source, a scout – might have given us some fraction of a chance against the trench of the dead that slowed our way. I had been so thrown off by Mother Pacifica's sneer that I didn't think to leave without paying. I set about my purse, digging at the pockets, fumbling to find the fifty quid he'd cheated me out of, as though I, not he, had committed the fraud. 'Oh,' said Mother Pacifica, just before he closed the door. 'Watch out for your friend.' And the door was shut before I could ask him to repeat himself.

By the time I returned home, my hair soaked through and smelling like a length of old fraying rope, I found Nat shaved and in a fresh shirt, his costume change for the dinner that had dropped clean out of my mind. We were half an hour late by the time we'd cut our diagonal path across the city. The address Nat's fellow pupil, Will Okoye, had texted over led us to a brick building in Bethnal Green behind the Museum of Childhood, the sort of building upon which the architect couldn't resist chiselling his name. We were let through a series of gates before we reached the right door, which was opened by a waif with Gibson girl hair who introduced herself as Will's girlfriend, Irma. Will came towards us smelling of garlic and fat and wiping his hands on his aproned thighs so he could take the bottle of Burgundy Nat had spent an afternoon researching.

'Bring some glasses, won't you, Irm?' Will asked Irma, as he conducted us inside. 'And the Chablis in the fridge?' He was tall, though not as tall as Nat, and always looked like he'd been carved in one piece. All his limbs were long and taut, his cheekbones high, his sharp jaw underlining his poise, his decisiveness. I would never have described him to anyone: not because of his good looks, but because of a nagging sense that any description would come across as an act of fetishism. Even the comparison of Will to a carving was probably a sign of suspect taste.

While Will asked Nat about the Faringdon Council case, I looked around the flat. The front door opened on to a sitting room, with a passage leading off at either end. The walls were painted a substantial Farrow & Ball kind of green and the charcoal-coloured couch was firm when I tried it. A framed print on the walls advertised an exhibition of sketches at the Musée Picasso in Paris. There were no signs of living: no half-opened letters, no receipts, no library books laid face down on the table, no crumpled shopping bags or hairpins. The immaculate edition of Mapplethorpe photographs on the low coffee table was the only sign that someone had been here before we arrived; otherwise, it was as clean as a set before a shoot. Seen in another light, I thought, the flat was indiscreet: it gave away its owner's compulsion for the discretion of surfaces. Its reticence, its intentionality were Will's absolutely: the keys in the ceramic bowl on the wooden sideboard, next to the pleated dahlias, and the record player.

Will stopped in the middle of whatever he was saying to Nat to ask, 'Are you having trouble with the bottle, Irma?'

'Shit,' Irma said from the kitchen, and then raised her voice, 'Coming!'

'You haven't corked it?' said Will.

Irma came in carrying several glasses upside down so that their stems sprouted from between her fingers and their bases overlapped in her palm. 'You never trust me, William,' she pouted.

There was barely any trace of Irma in the flat. When I went to the bathroom, I saw three or four hair products on the rim of the shower and a cloth bag of make-up, but no razor, no tampons, no hairs knotted in the shower drain. By then I was sure that Irma was the sort of free spirit who left her clothes wherever she took them off; the sort of girl who forgot the coffee she'd just made, and called her friend halfway through a film.

'How does he pay for it?' I asked Nat later on the Central line towards home. 'The organic meat, his furniture, the wine.'

'The fuck I know,' said Nat, 'but he spends hardly anything. Doesn't go out for lunch, drinks the chambers' coffee.'

I suspected Will of saving every cheque he had ever been given on his birthday, after graduating, as payment for part-time or seasonal work. That he had always lived in the

Not Now none of us knew how to recognize. And all the while he was saying *no*, he was thinking of what might be good enough, one day, to not regret: a list in his mind, a gold standard, which he refined and polished.

The wine tasted like clarinets. For half a glass, I did nothing but sip on it. Will, pleased, said it was called Le Meaulnes, like the novel. I liked his pleasure, the sudden smile that broke up his reserve. More wine was poured. When the men were well into their beating of the bounds, Irma and I turned to each other to exchange our origin stories. She and Will had met on a dating app, Irma said. Their first date was at the Barbican and they had liked each other immediately. Immediately there was chemistry, immediately the conversation took shape, took off, ran away with them. They had gone back to her house, the house owned by her parents in Maida Vale, since her mother and father were travelling at the time and she had no fear of running into them. I saw the coming farce: the tipsy couple raking open the door with the quivering key, the father reading his *Financial Times* by lamplight, an opera plot. (Will went to check on his lamb; Nat sat down politely beside us.) But no! Irma told the story all the way through successful coitus, the house's continued emptiness, brunch, a second date. Nat and I sat, half-embarrassed in the way that couples are after years together when they find themselves under the lamplight of sexual pleasure and are determined not to be prudish. I wanted to ask Irma if Will had actually been drunk since I couldn't imagine him in a state of disorder. Even his passions, I thought, must be careful. When he fell, it was because he'd chosen to.

We smelled the oven open, we heard the plates unstacked, laid on the round table in the centre of the kitchen.

'Where did you live before this, Irma?' Nat asked as we walked through together. He meant, 'Where is your accent from?'

'Irma's from Mexico,' said Will.

Here, I thought as I took my seat, was another peripheral factor.

'Mexico City,' corrected Irma.

Here was the mask of the city slipping off. Only London wasn't a city, it was a library of cities: it contained whole other cities in miniature, excerpted or condensed, proportionately scaled to some formula beyond my calculation. It contained Paris; it contained Berlin. It contained a fraction of Cairo, a sliver of Beirut, a corner of Kyiv. How else could I make sense of the sheer number of Mexicans emerging from its terraces, alleys and doorways? Nat must have felt each ricochet in my mind because his not looking at me said, sharply, *No*.

'And your parents live in London?' I asked Irma, politely.

'Irma's parents are plastic surgeons,' said Will, setting plates in front of us. 'Both of them.'

Irma was not at all embarrassed by this. Irma had accepted the need for plastic surgeons, though she herself would never require their services. Then again, her parents might have done something to make her pretty, bird-like face: they might have said to themselves, we did it very well the first time, but our work is not quite finished. She'll thank us later, when she is sleeping with a handsome London barrister and living in Bethnal Green.

'Mexico City is very sophisticated,' said Irma so that it was clear that 'sophisticated' meant 'dissatisfied'. 'My father's mother and sister are both psychoanalysts. One is a classic Freudian, the other follows Klein.' So Irma, we concluded, was rich. Her richness allowed her to study fashion at Saint Martins, but she was so sparrow-like we couldn't judge her for it. Even sparrows must live, and sparrows find bills impossible. They must find their sparrowhawks, and keep them fed and contented, too heavy to hunt.

The lamb Will prepared was tender enough to weep when he carved it.

'Will knows I like blood in my meat,' said Irma.

'Mexico might be sophisticated,' Will said, 'but Irma is a barbarian.'

Irma smiled gruesomely, purple-mouthed. 'I said Mexico City, not Mexico,' she said. 'There's a difference.' The Burgundy had been opened. 'Will likes barbarians,' Irma said. They were still new enough together to be compelled to explain each other, to tell each other's biographies to visitors.

'I'd love to go to Mexico,' I told Irma. Nat continued to eat, doggedly; it was how he would bear me when we were old.

'Will won't come,' said Irma. 'He's afraid of flying.'

But Will was unembarrassed. 'Call me a coward,' he said, 'but machines weighing over three hundred tonnes were not meant to be in the air. The last time I flew, we were halfway into the flight before the pilot announced that we'd been within two kilometres of colliding with another aeroplane. *Two kilometres.*'

'Christ,' said Nat, a nervous flier who pretended he wasn't.

'So because of this we hardly go anywhere,' complained Irma over lean crossed arms.

'We travel by Eurostar,' Will objected. 'We take the ferry.'

'The ferry, the ferry,' said Irma. 'You need an extra week just to get where you want to go.'

When I asked Irma if she missed Mexico, she said, 'How

can I when my family is always coming here? My cousin Alejandro is coming next week and he's a real pain in the arse. When he was little, he lived with my grandparents and they spoiled him, they even let him have his own TV so he could watch *The Simpsons* while we went to church. And now? Now nothing's good enough for Alejandro: his girlfriend, his job, his apartment, everything's a disappointment. But does he do anything to change it? Anyway, I go home once or twice a year,' she continued. 'If I'm lucky, I miss an earthquake. I'd rather have been born in Paris. A Mexican passport takes you nowhere.'

'South African passports too,' I said, but Irma was not listening to me; she was looking at her lamb, teasing it apart as if trying to decide whether it was bloody enough.

'It's not that I don't want to go,' Will was explaining to Nat. 'It's that when we do go, it should be done properly.'

'Did you study in Mexico before you came to London?' I asked. All these questions were permitted, friendly, safe, even if they bored lovely Irma.

'I studied medicine at UNAM—' She saw my surprise. 'My parents said if I passed medicine, they'd let me do what I liked. But Margaret – is it Margaret?'

'Margit.'

'Let me tell you, Margaret, it was horrible. All those corpses. I wanted to dress them up. Even the fat ones, which made it so hard to get to the organs – you should see the layers of fat, white and creamy and oily, and you have to keep cutting, keep keep cutting – I thought the whole time what I would put on them, what would suit their morphology.'

Nat put down his knife and fork.

'I didn't say anything,' I said while Nat pressed his linen

napkin neatly to his mouth. Will and Irma waited expectantly for him to explain.

'Margit is macabre,' he said, folding his napkin. 'She's become infatuated with it,' he continued, and I understood that this was his way of punishing me for my straying attention, for that deflected kiss.

'Serial killers?' Will asked, filling our glasses diplomatically. 'Women found in suitcases?'

'Oh my god,' said Irma in disgust.

'She's wetting her pants that you're from Mexico,' Nat said to Irma. 'She's obsessed with a Mexican crime.'

'Which one?' said Irma, as though she were asking where he got off the Tube. Nat waited pointedly for me to speak, for me to claim the paternity of the deformed offspring he'd left for me on a bare stage. But I was tired of theatrical interrogations, and Mother Pacifica was still a fresh paper cut between my fingers, a bluebottle sting under my heel.

'The Case of the Disappearing Students,' said Nat. 'Don't let her ask you any more questions, Irma, she has a notebook. She has diagrams.'

But Irma didn't seem to mind. '*Los normalistas?*' she said, with the mild surprise of someone who has lifted a potted plant and found her hands closing on a collar of snails. 'My friends were always going to those manifestations. It made them very cynical. One dropped out of his studies. The others got depressed. I believe you can either be political and lose your mind or you can live your life. The government will do what they will do.'

She delivered her opinion with such certainty that I watched Nat and Will to see if they were drawing the only conclusion there could be: that Irma could stand apart from the tedium of politics because her parents were plastic surgeons. That no one would tell her not to be stupid because her richness and prettiness exempted her from critique. Instead, Will turned to me and asked, 'Why Mexico? What is it about this particular series of events?'

'That's like asking a painter why he chooses his subject,' I said, hoping the conversation would blow over, blow out, like that floating, flaming newspaper my neighbour's children set alight.

'Is it?' Will said, his expression flickering between amusement and disgust. It wasn't going to blow over. Nat was looking the other way but I could hear the high pitch of his attention, like pylons in the bush.

'I suppose,' I said slowly, laying down my knife and fork, waiting for an answer to come to me, some adequate phrase. 'I suppose—'

'I mean, you're South African, aren't you?' Will said. 'Doesn't your country have its own fucked-up traumas to scrapbook?'

'God, gender,' I said, and here I was on safer ground.

'Gender?' Nat said.

'Scrapbooking,' I said, 'implies a female trivialization of significant historical – i.e. masculine – events. Back me up, Irma,' I said, but she shrugged. She seemed to find arguments, like politics, a waste of energy. 'Scrapbooks are ephemeral. Banal, sentimental, personal.'

The last time I had visited Nina's classroom – visits that were always embarrassing somehow, because I was seeing her public self, the Nina everyone else had to interpret without the allowances I gave her – I recognized each of the old posters, the corners curling against the drawing pins, including the one with the quotation by Rebecca West which said *Idiocy is the female defect*. She had pinned it up between vague reproductions of Brontë, Eliot and Woolf. The quotation continued: *Intent on their private lives, women follow their fate through a darkness deep as that cast by malformed cells in the brain.* I had never known what to make of the quotation. It was a strange thing to put in front of clever girls.

But Will was undeterred. 'Wasn't there something not too long ago?' he said. 'Not scrapbooking – South Africa. I remember talking about it in politics when I was at school. The name's on the tip of my tongue. Mm,' he said. 'It began with a Mm, marry, mari, Marietta—' He took his phone from the counter behind him and, resting his elbows on the table, began to type. He squinted like a man untying a knot in a fine gold chain. 'Yes,' he said. 'Here it is. Not Marietta – Marikana. The Marikana massacre. The sixteenth of August 2012. "The most lethal use of force" by the South African police since 1976, widely compared to the Sharpeville massacre of 1960.'

'I wasn't there,' I said.

'What, Sharpeville?' said Nat, sticking his fork prongs back into the lamb with bravado.

What do you know about Sharpeville? I wanted to hiss.

'Thirty-four people killed,' Will continued. 'Seventy-eight injured. Wildcat strike – *British*-owned platinum mine—' he said with exaggerated significance, as though the four of us were shareholders. 'The police suspected of doctoring photographs, of placing weapons in the hands of dead miners, who were greedy enough to want to be paid £600 a month for the pleasure of toiling in the bowels of the earth day after day and dying of tuberculosis at 45 instead of the £220 they had been getting for years. Then, drum roll please, strikers rounded up and accused of murder. *And*, and this is the kicker,' he said, 'and I quote, "Following the incident the spot price for platinum rose on world commodity markets." What's not to like? Where's your patriotism?'

What could I say? You develop a certain thickness to the country of your birth, a scab, an indifference equal to its indifference towards you. Like the stories your grandfather tells year after year, it fails to stir your imagination.

'It's not a question of patriotism,' I said. 'We all agree, I think, that patriotism is bullshit.'

'I suppose I want to ask,' Will said, 'and sorry Margit, I don't mean this to be unnecessarily combative, but what's your stake? I mean, where's your sense of history?'

Let me tell you about history, I wanted to say. History is a prefabricated classroom ruled by a tired woman in her late fifties. Clean-faced Mrs Muir, who wears men's clothes too large for her, loose shirts in tacky florals and shorts with elastic waists, and her coarse hair dyed black and cut into a pine cone. She is married to a Unitarian minister, a man of exquisite manners who is good at his job but emotionally fragile. She teaches us for years because there is a shortage of history teachers. Because no one wants to do history now – history's a drag, full of excuses, we're about the future, the children of the rainbow nation. Still, she teaches us with a weariness that impresses us. We study World War II every year until we can recite the dates from the annexation of the Sudetenland up to the implementation of blitzkrieg tactics by heart. We can interpret all varieties of Nazi propaganda and can hold forth on the devaluation of the German mark, though we know nothing about Hitler's Night and Fog directive. Nor do we know about the two thousand forced disappearances in our own country, although we do apartheid every year, too – *do*, as though it could be *done with* – as though the Truth and Reconciliation Commission hadn't just wrapped up its findings, as though we hadn't worn bonnets and wide-brimmed hats and carried wooden muskets as children, re-enacting the Battle of Blood River and regretting the death of Piet Retief at the hands of the treacherous Dingane. Mrs Muir must have despaired at our moral incompetence. But then, that is what history at sixteen and seventeen is like, thinking not of Botha, the reptilian former president, dying by degrees in his beachside villa a few hours east along the coast, but of the golden scent of Johan van Rensburg's aftershave wafting from where he sits loosely in front of you. When Mrs Muir loses her temper, she slams the door of the prefabricated classroom behind her in a way that moves us. She has no interest in being professional; she cries in front of us more than once. Not at us, or our thickheadedness, but because of the bomb, the fickleness of the Western powers, Sharpeville. She might have cried also over the fragility of her husband the Unitarian minister, or over the narrowness of her life teaching history to cardboard minds. She might have cried over her country's promise and promises, cut shorter every day, trimmed, economized, sold.

27

London in October: Virginia creepers turning gory, empty packs of cigarettes sticking to the pavement, old men with wrecked faces under bus shelters. On my twenty-seventh birthday, Nat was in court. He was in such a rush to leave the flat that he forgot his phone, leaving it on the kitchen table playing Waylon Jennings. I'd taken the day off from endoscopy and listened to the whole of *Ladies Love Outlaws*. He was a bouquet-buying species, Nat, but he showed up at eight that evening with his hands empty and his mood scraping the barrel. We walked up to West Hampstead for tapas, up Iverson Road, and I couldn't decide whether I was happy that Nat's sense of duty had beaten his exhaustion, or glum that any celebration had to be claimed at the expense of his good manners. The weather was drippy and the streets empty: there was no heart in any of it. It was like Valentine's Day, seeing couples through the windows, dressed up with nothing to say, the standardized rituals of pleasure pleasing no one. Few men ever bought a woman a necklace she liked.

Your present is at home, Nat told me, when we knocked our glasses together. The wine helped. Our wrinkled lips stained at the same rate. The client of one of the cases Nat was observing was a real bastard, he told me; every court appearance was a chore. The man had no gift for making the best of a bad situation. He was bigoted, deliberately inflammatory, and aggravated every judge he'd ever stood before. The lead counsel was ready to bash her head in at the bench. It'd be technicalities or nothing that got this dickhead off. It was all down to Nat's research – to his eye for loopholes – and he was starting to sweat under the pressure. The sheer boredom of the documents he had to read was interfering with his circadian rhythms. Whenever Nat talked about his job, I wanted to ask, 'Are you happy now?' but I never did.

We ordered olives, boquerones, tuna, patatas bravas, Manchego. When the bill came, he asked me how I'd spent my birthday and I told him I Marie Kondo'd the kitchen cabinets. Meat thermometers did not spark joy. Neither did the dregs of three different bags of whole coffee beans, the white paprika, our can opener or the purple spatula. I didn't tell him that I'd drunk the end of last year's sloe gin and looked through every message on his phone, opened his banking app, scrolled through his recent photographs, and examined his inbox for the months of August, September and October. There was something attractive about the distance between his virtual and my physical self: some electric estrangement that didn't exist when we were in the same room. We walked back to Kilburn with a tarta de Santiago in a plastic bag hanging from the arm Nat had draped across my shoulders like a red velvet curtain in a theatre. My arm was just above his waist and we rattled against each other whenever we lost our step. At home, he opened a bottle of Crémant, and we sat on the couch eating our tart off saucers with teaspoons.

'Where's my present?' I asked, because there are never enough ribbons to cut.

'It's not quite right,' he said, scraping the saucer with his teaspoon, so I knew he was feeling the wine. 'Forget I said anything,' he said, frowning, chewing, and then added, mostly to himself, 'It's no good.'

'No good?' I repeated.

'No,' he said, and then, with the finger-wagging mock pomposity of a children's dentist, 'not good for you.'

'What the hell does that mean?' I said.

'God, Margit,' he said sharply. 'It means that I'm tired of hearing you talk about it.' I could tell from the look on his face he hadn't meant to be so loud, so patriarchal, but he'd still got those notes in him; they were there for good now, part of his range. The air spiked. I breathed small shallow breaths so it didn't stick me. 'The real present,' he said, after a beat, in an easier voice, 'is a bank holiday in Budapest. Pastries at the Gerbeaud, a visit to the House of Terror – you'll love it.'

I said nothing, knowing that every word, however slight, added to the scale. He left and came back with a record to thread on to his record player. He let Skip James make his apology for him, and who could refuse Skip James and his Delta sincerity? We sat against each other on the couch, and he stroked my leg with his fingertips, stroking against the grain, the way you comb out your hair when it is knotted with seawater and sand. He was quiet with the heaviness of the music, as if it were honestly his. When our mouths opened against each other, it was with the same heaviness hatched between us. As though we were enemies and every step we took towards each other was against our best instincts. It hadn't been this good for a year. It might never have been so good, so wretched.

In the morning, Nat's concession sat on the kitchen table, wrapped in brown paper. Inside, I found the *History of the Conquest of Mexico: With a Preliminary View of the Ancient Mexican Civilization, and the Life of the Conqueror, Hernando Cortés*, in two volumes, by William Hickling Prescott. On the flyleaf, in pencil, was written *2 vols, £6*. Ugly, musty, almost furred, these were the kind of books picked up at auctions by the kilogram, bought by certain gastropubs for the colour of their boards and arranged by the interior decorator, alongside *The ABC of Engineering, Elementary Physics* and *The Flora of Lincolnshire*. In past years, he'd given me cooking lessons and leather shoes and tickets to plays he saw advertised on the Underground. He had turned a new leaf. This was something he must have found in the window of an Oxfam: a sign of spontaneity, or impulsiveness, or desperation, a substitute – something to hand over while Budapest took shape. I kept an eye on them while I boiled the kettle. The books stayed put, smelling of church jumble sales and old attics turned out. Nat had said nothing about his outburst the night before, but he was evidently full of regret, sorry enough to relent and let me get my hands on what looked like the dullest read in North London. For his sake, I picked up the first volume, skipped the preface, and read the opening sentence:

Of all that extensive empire which once acknowledged the authority of Spain in the New World, no portion, for interest and importance, can be compared with Mexico;—and this equally, whether we consider the variety of its soil and climate; the inexhaustible stores of its mineral wealth; its scenery, grand and picturesque beyond example; the character of its ancient inhabitants, not only far surpassing in intelligence that of the other North American races, but reminding us, by their monuments, of the primitive civilisation of Egypt and Hindostan; and lastly, the peculiar circumstances of its Conquest, adventurous and romantic as any legend devised by Norman or Italian bard of chivalry.

The photograph of the author I found on the Internet showed a pair of deep-set, faulty, delicate, even melancholy eyes set off by a resolute chin and a Roman nose. Prescott, I learned (b. Salem, Mass., 1796 – d. Boston, 1859), was a man with the bad luck of having a photographic memory and poor eyes, those melancholy eyes faulty not from birth but ruined after an injury inflicted by a crust of bread thrown in a Harvard food fight. After producing, half-blind, a series of admired histories, Prescott had been invited to write a history of the Mexican–American War. He turned the invitation down, uninterested in writing about contemporary events. Instead, he produced the *History of the Conquest of Mexico*, which was considered his greatest literary accomplishment, these homely brown books now weighing down my kitchen table with their whiff of shillings and ha'pennies. Ten hours later, when Nat came home scowling, damp and cross, having been caught without his umbrella, I was on the couch. 'Listen to this,' I said. 'Prescott on Cortés:

'There are some hardy natures that require the heats of excited action to unfold their energies; like the plants which, closed to the mild influence of a temperate latitude, come to their full growth, and give forth their fruits, only in the burning atmosphere of the tropics.

'Only in the burning atmosphere of the tropics,' I repeated, satisfied. Nat pulled at his tie. 'I knew it,' he said. 'I knew it was a bad idea.'

28

'Think of it like a PhD,' I said at King's Cross, Prescott in hand, 'like Harry's girlfriend at King's.'

'Yes, and Harry says if he ever hears Anya say another word about Beckett,' Nat said, 'he's going on Tinder.'

We were to take the 10:51 to Cambridge and arrive just before lunch. I could imagine standing under the whorl of King's Cross at the end of time. It was the sort of place where we'd wait with all our earthly possessions, under the chequered light, staring up at the boards. Maybe at the end of time the boards would fail with no one to programme them, but even then, I thought, we'd still be staring upwards, under this dome, with this same calibration of anticipation and despair.

'The alternative,' I said, 'is to have no interests and spend your weekends watching *Bake Off*.'

'The alternative,' Nat replied, 'is to have a normal range of interests, where you leave the house, and talk about what you're watching on TV, and where you'll go for brunch, and how much you hate Brexit *or*,' he continued, just as I was about to say how dull that sounded, '*or* just get on with it. Learn to cycle. Visit Reykjavík. Find a real job.'

But what if this is my real job? I wanted to say to him.

Unpaid, unnoticed – my vocation. Why was it any less real than wearing a wig and quarrelling for a living?

'And make sure you don't read in front of my mother,' Nat said over his shoulder as we went through the ticket barrier. 'She hates it when people close themselves off.'

What could I say? There was something about Nat when he disapproved of me, some armoured self-assurance, some pride, that suited him. He came up to his full height and I wanted to throw myself at him, like a swimmer pounding on the shore, demanding to be let onto land.

29

The Garsides' home, a terraced house in north Cambridge, was filled with books. There were cookbooks in the kitchen, where we ate around an unvarnished wooden table, and where the light from the garden coming through the glassy extension was discreet and expensive, a cashmere light, pearled and fluted. There were novels in the hall and histories in the sitting room, and both favoured the Second World War, its large battles and secret assignations. Nat's white-haired father, Oliver, was born in bomb-struck London, and the war was his family romance. But even with a house full of books, I had never seen a member of the family open one. Not covertly pinched from a shelf on a walk to the upstairs toilet; not even at Christmas between tipsy brunch and boozy dinner when everyone was stupefied and mush-mouthed. The telly would be on in the sitting room and the radio would be on in the kitchen, while Oliver fretted and sipped over the cooking.

Now, just when I thought it was safe to reach into my holdall for all those pounds of Prescott, Claudia came to sit by me with her fine-rimmed reading glasses at the end of her nose, and her phone held out at arm's length while she peered at it, first over her glasses, and then through them, back and forth, sharp as a blackbird. 'Margit, darling, you're young,' she said, 'can you tell me what a Google Alert is? I find I'm the last to know what anyone is doing. Nat's no use at all,' she interrupted me when I began to suggest she ask him. 'He never answers my questions. Or rather he rephrases my questions so I can't quite recognize them. Sophist.'

'Barrister,' said Nat from the other couch.

Claudia, just retired from her position as the CEO of an educational trust, was ferocious with energy. Without an assistant, or a synced calendar, or meetings over lunch, she was no longer expected to whip others into shape, to get results. She still rose at five, we learned the next morning from her footsteps on the stairs, and from the muffled sounds of the kettle and Radio 3; she still read *The Times* over her coffee. She had long ago reached the age where you attributed your success to your personal habits. 'Dear Margit,' she said whenever she met me, as though she was addressing one last letter. 'Dear, dear Margit.'

'She was such a surprise,' I imagined her saying to her friends. 'Nat has always gone in for English roses. Not very ambitious, I'm afraid, dear Margit.'

'Now, Margit.' She squared herself to me. 'How is the job hunt? You must be dreadfully bored.' She meant, 'You are taking your time.'

Aggie, the family's black French bulldog, came towards us, snuffling laboriously through the flat holes of her nose, her bat-winged ears swivelling to catch stray affection. She stood at my feet, her head cocked. 'Aggie adores you, doesn't she?' said Claudia. 'I'm afraid we're going to have to get her glaucoma checked again.' There was a desperate look in Aggie's tiger-eye marbles, as if she knew I couldn't stand her.

The morbid motor of her breath, her anxious attention, the worried creases between her enormous ears, alert as a broken umbrella, the ladder of her raisin-sized nipples. I could smell her fish breath wheezing between her needle-like teeth.

'Did you know most French bulldogs are incapable of reproducing?' I said to Nat after we married. 'That the bitches are artificially inseminated, like turkeys? That most of them are delivered by caesarean because their heads are bred too big for their mothers' hips?'

When we came back from Cambridge, our neighbour and his family were gone. The garden was bare. The tools had been removed or packed away, the wood stacked against the fence. There were no plastic plates, or half-buried forks, or deflated footballs on the scragged lawn. The table and chairs remained, but they'd been washed and brought under shelter. Come to think of it, I hadn't seen my neighbour for a while. It had been some time since he had sat outside with his pipe. Was disappearance contagious? I wondered. Could it travel through the air like clouds of ash? Or like particles of radiation that seep into drinking water and common air, coating fingertips and tongues with omnivorous atoms, eating away into the outlines of things? Perhaps it was like leprosy, which the visiting nuns of Saint Boniface's Hospital in Tanzania had informed us in Grade 6 had not been fully eradicated, although it was different from how people imagined it, and the vanished limbs, the missing nose or fingers, did not drop off in the course of the disease (as was commonly thought) but were lost through nerve damage and infection, through amputation, and even reabsorption.

If they had been reabsorbed, the missing forty-three, what ground was ready for them? What body, what building was hungry enough to take them in? According to William Hickling Prescott, Cortés's soldiers lost themselves in halls dimpled with empty eye sockets and accented with long, grinning cornices of teeth, counting at least one hundred and thirty-six thousand skulls embedded in the walls and lintels and door frames of the sacrificial temples of their enemies. Then again, as Prescott observed, they were the children of the Spanish Inquisition, familiar with the rack and the screw, the severed head and the pyre. In later centuries, their Czech brothers in Christ thought nothing of decorating a provincial chapel with similar and more extravagant touches (or so Nat told me, having been to Sedlec years ago on a lads' weekend): ribbons of skulls, chandeliers in bone, symbols spelled out in femurs and humeri, a macabre if subtle tribute to whatever horrors the conquistadors had seen in the temple of Huitzilopochtli and claimed to despise.

Then again, perhaps they were beyond incorporation, those unknowable forty-three. Perhaps they had been seen in certain circles as signs of infection, like the lesions and numbed limbs belonging to the lepers of Saint Boniface's Hospital in Tanzania, whose nuns, however good, frightened us with their matter-of-factness, their insistence on the carbolic cleanliness of exposing old myths to the light. When the infection goes too far, they had said, sometimes you have to cut it off to spare it from contaminating the rest of the body. Such phrases, or phrases like them, might have travelled along certain wires, been uttered into certain private or disposable phones, evidence that metaphors can have concrete results.

Whatever Aurelia Olivera Cassou had to say about it, each analogy felt like a spade in the ground, a shovelful of debris lifted clear of the heap. It had been two weeks since I'd left her behind on the library terrace and still I'd heard nothing from Regan. *Call me when you get this*, I texted. Also: *You ok?* But a text is nothing more than a scrap of paper left in the crevice of a wall, or a radio frequency sent into outer space: a way of figuring out what we need to say to ourselves. There was no sign she'd read my messages, no footprints in the sand proved her attention had been, however briefly, caught. She was out with a new lover. She had lost her phone. She was out of data. She was out of time. She was undercover. She was underwater. She had lost her head. Someone had taken her head. Someone had cut off her fingers. She would wash up on the Isle of Wight; her tattoos would be her identification and her epitaph. *Call me*, I texted, again.

30

Although Nat called her his cousin, Lucy was the daughter
of his godmother, Diana, a friend of Claudia's from their
Wiltshire convent school days. Diana had been a part-time
model in Soho for a year or two before she married, and she
was still tall and slim, velvet-eyed, living the afterlife of a great
beauty. 'She thinks Africa is a country,' Claudia whispered in
my ear the first time she introduced me to her schoolfriend.

Lucy was nothing like her mother. She had a first in maths
from Cambridge and, ten years after her finals, this coup had
suffered no erosion. 'I work in compliance at Goldman's,' she
told me at the table overlooking the dark, sticky South Bank.
'Do you know what that is?'

We had been eight minutes late to meet Lucy at the BFI for
a film, and as soon as Nat and I walked through the doors, I
recognized from our wedding photographs the sharp woman
with the decisive haircut sitting at a table with her upturned
hand in the grasp of a slight, serious man drawing mesmeric
circles on her palm with his index finger.

'Goldman Sachs?' I said.

'Compliance,' she said.

'It definitely doesn't mean she does what I say,' said the man, dropping her hand. His name was Joe.

'It's regulatory,' she said, ignoring him. 'We manage risk.'

Five feet tall with arched ankle boots, Lucy was a woman whose purse held nothing more than her phone and her keys, sleeping with a man in jeans and Converse. Joe's round wire-frame glasses and knit cap rolled up at the sides made him look like a scholarly North Sea fisherman. Beneath the cap, his head would be shaved to the same length as his five o'clock shadow to hide the loss of his hair. She'd imagine him unconventional because he didn't think about stocks or know how to drive.

Neither of them asked what I did and I didn't mind, but I smelled a thicker hint of ambition on Nat. There was a tightness to his limbs, an eagerness to lay his life out when the time came. Lucy described the long hours, the endless paperwork, and yes, the money was good, and the benefits were good, but work–life balance was rubbish, interrupted Joe, and Lucy objected by saying there were no jobs going now where the work–life balance was good unless you were a teacher in a nursery school or worked in a shop, and either way your brain regressed.

'What about librarians?' said Joe.

'Joe,' said Lucy, 'there are like five librarians in London and they're married to brain surgeons or how else do they pay their mortgage?'

Lucy knew the price of everything. Still, I remembered the story of the holiday to France with Nat's family after Lucy's father left Diana, and how Lucy had shaved her entire body, even down there, with a cheap razor and cried in the swimming pool from how much the chemicals stung. People don't come from nowhere.

'Claudia says you're on the Elliott inquiry,' she said to Nat.

'She shouldn't have said anything,' said Nat, pleased. 'I'm very minor. I type out notes.'

'Bullshit,' said Lucy. 'You're researching. You write arguments.'

'I *draft* arguments,' he said.

Joe had lost interest. His thumbs were like small hammers on the dulcimer of his phone. It got to me, the careless way he sat there in his rolled-up cap.

'Joe,' said Lucy, 'you're being antisocial.'

Joe finished typing his sentence and laid the phone down on the table, unhumiliated.

'Face down,' she said.

'It'll scratch the screen,' he said, and compromised by sliding it down the tight front pocket of his jeans.

I wanted to shake him until his face took on some kind of expression.

'Ten minutes,' he said, catching Lucy's wrist and bending it so he could read her watch. 'Should we refuel?'

Nat volunteered to foot the bill and Lucy went with him to the bar because she couldn't decide on a red. In their absence, Joe picked up his phone.

'Do you work at a bank too?' I asked Joe. He snorted.

'I'd rather kill myself,' he said.

A sharp, thorny dislike was growing in my ribcage – those two-inch-long white thorns that grow on the acacia tree which Shaka, king of the Zulus, ordered his impi to crush with their bare feet in order to harden their soles.

'And what do you do to avoid killing yourself?' I said, which bought enough of his attention.

'Computers,' he said. 'My social awkwardness is genuine.'

165

I'd hate to think it was a pose, I thought. The self-consciousness of his style of conversation, the self-consciousness he sparked in me, got on my nerves. The only way to treat men like Joe was with the white thorns of the acacia tree.

'Joe's a forensic architect,' said Lucy, catching our conversation by the tail. She leaned over the table under the storm cloud of her grey wrap, pushing Joe's pint towards him, her neat fingers grasping the rounded bowl of her large wine glass. 'They reconstruct trauma centres: prisons in Syria, bombed hospitals,' said Lucy. 'Should we go in? I hate rushing into a cinema. Joe calls it a soup. They put everything in, building plans, surveys, photographs, witness statements, videos—'

'Into the cinema?' said Nat.

'The trauma centres,' said Lucy.

'I've never called it a soup,' said Joe, gathering his pint and loping after her. 'I object to your metaphor.'

'Okay, Jesus, Joe, you object to my metaphor,' said Lucy. 'By the way,' she said over her shoulder to us, 'you know this is like three hours long, don't you?'

'Are you stuck with interiors?' I asked Joe, from where I stood at his elbow. 'Or can you reconstruct what happens *between* buildings?'

We waited to show our tickets to the attendant, a young, personable Irishman, saving up, sure, to buy his first proper camera. With each rip of a ticket, he became more courtly, more possessive, as if it were his own film we were about to see. In the theatre, Nat strained his eyes at the glossy brochure of film showings he had found on his seat. 'It's only 155 minutes,' he whispered apologetically.

'You won't notice it,' Joe leaned forward and said to Nat.

'It's a complete experience. I've seen it once a year, every year since 2003. I almost studied Russian at university because of this film. Lucy's never seen it. I've been badgering her to watch *Stalker* since we met.' Lucy sat placidly on Joe's right. ('Who knew she had the patience for foreign film?' Nat said later as we walked towards Waterloo.)

When the credits began, large yellow Cyrillic letters bubbling over colourless images, my heart sank along with the overhead lights. Old movies had that effect on me: the graininess of them, the audience's pretence at being transfigured, was depressing. From minute to minute, *Stalker* got uglier: oily rain, unused tankers, everything broken and breaking down. And yet there sat Joe, the slackness on his face gone, the fidgeting of his fingers gone, intent on the ugliness, on the wandering back and forth, on the dialogue that went nowhere, on the awful screeching wife with her ugly mannish hair.

After a while, I wondered: *could* he reconstruct what happened between buildings? It was almost a vibration between my legs, the fact that Joe was so close, that his left arm was just there by my right arm, and that at the end of that arm was his wrist and his hand and his fingers, and those fingers could tap his way into something, could assemble something, could uncover something. I wanted to tell him things I knew: that I'd recognized one of Lucian Freud's models on the street because of her cat eyes, that planes occasionally bump rare paintings from their hold in favour of prizewinning racehorses, that in New York there is a warehouse full of damaged art which can be neither exhibited nor destroyed. But I could tell he was a man who only listened if your investment was worth it, and I couldn't prove I had the funds. On the screen, ugly men in dirty coats went on jumping on and off their cars and trams, driving on and off the train lines, until they got to the place with the crooked cables they'd been trying to reach. It didn't matter that the film was in colour now; there were still filthy bubbles on the river and needles and syringes in the stream, coins, papers.

I looked sideways at Joe, who was sitting so still he seemed to have stopped breathing. He'd forgotten his pint, growing warm in the seat's cup holder. Would he mind if I leaned in and whispered very, very softly, to ask, 'What kind of information do you need?' and 'How much does it cost?' and 'Do you have any contacts in the Mexican government?' and 'How do you find your witnesses?' All the while the awful noise of the film continued, the ratcheting, shunting trains, the jangling, humming, quivering wires, the sound of slate on slate, of breaking teeth, of toenails on cement, the metallic clicks, the dripping water.

When the film was over, Joe told us that they had filmed *Stalker* three times: once, because the original footage was damaged, and then they had to do it again, and the director kept falling out with the crew. It was filmed, he said, in Estonia near a chemical plant, and everyone spent so much time in the filthy river that the director, Tarkovsky, eventually died of lung cancer, as did his wife and one of the actors. We didn't ask for any of this information, but you couldn't stop him – he seemed to know everything there was about the making of the film. When I returned from the toilet, I was determined to interrupt, to ask Joe for information I could do something with, rather than trivia about film history and long Russian patronymics and conspiracy theories about the KGB. But Nat was waiting for me by the stairs alone. Lucy had an early morning, he explained, sent her apologies, etcetera, but I wondered if they were so turned on by the filth of the polluted rivers of Estonia and by that shunting sound of the train that they'd hired a cab with Lucy's money, the money that made Joe a little sick but also grateful, returning in hot haste to the flat paid for by her compliance.

31

I began to think if you typed anyone's name into YouTube, they'd come up like a genie from a lamp. Attorney General Jesús Murillo Karam appeared, in his blue pinstriped suit and claret-coloured tie. I'd imagined a tall, hook-nosed man, a brooding spectre, a retired general, but his skin was like old parchment, the dome of his head was balding and pouches hung under his eyes. He looked like a mob boss, like a chief of police, like a middle-aged poet. When the camera drew back, you could see that the prosecutor was standing with his weight on his back foot. His trousers were made for the belly, not for the leg he put forward as a small but noticeable assertion. When he spoke, his lips parted to reveal a row of pearly teeth. According to YouTube, over two million people had watched the Attorney General delivering his account of the Historical Truth, streamed live on 7 November 2014 under the aegis of the President (comments disabled). Of the many words Murillo Karam spoke, I understood only *palabras*, *complicado*, *testimonios* and *medio de la noche*, or maybe it was *medianoche*.

His eyebrows were little pelts, stroked against the grain. The flag at his left was at rest, the eagle biting the back of a snake's head, the eagle's claws clutching the snake's coils, a badge of the Attorney General's ruthlessness, his willingness to pursue his enemies, and to cut them off, even at risk to himself. Still, the Attorney General was not wholly able to control the show. From time to time, PowerPoint stalled, or the video he wished to address was slow to appear. He paused, looking meaningfully but wearily out at those who had failed him. His hands flapped palm up as if to say, 'Where the hell is it?' or, 'And now?' as he looked around him, as if to say, '*This* is what I have to put up with.'

He resumed: testimonies, maps, aerial shots of hills thickly crowded with scrubby trees. The videos showed the accused – downcast men with blurred faces, apparently corrupt local police officers and depraved members of the local cartel, Guerreros Unidos, all of whom folded immediately – speaking reluctantly in response to emphatic questions in rooms where crucifixes were hung high on the wall. These confessions alternated with footage of men in white forensic suits steadily searching the rubbish tip at Cocula with who knows how much suspicion that their work was fruitless; they were used to foregone conclusions, perhaps, disillusioned, but then again there was the doctor's bill; depressed, maybe, and drinking too much at the end of every shift. As befitted an official investigation, the ground was divided into squares marked by white string and ornamented with scraping tools, brown bags, plastic gloves, numbered identification markers, etcetera. The camera zoomed in close on grubby objects I couldn't quite decipher, but I thought I recognized teeth. The evidence was safely packed away in marked crates with yellow lids.

When the Attorney General was through, he closed his file

and handed it with ceremony to an unseen aide, the slight but exquisite weight of his eyelids causing them to droop momentarily as if to say, 'How this weighs on me' or, 'Guard this with your life.' He looked as if, even while he took the stage, he was in the battle for his own inner life, which he waged by thinking of Florence, perhaps, by remembering certain rooms in the Uffizi, which he had been fortunate enough to visit on more than one occasion. His eyebrows rose slightly when the convenor announced that they would take questions, as though he was acknowledging his own impeccable behaviour in condescending to this manifestation of his weary generosity. When the questions began, the camera swivelled so that we saw what the Attorney General had been looking at during his presentation: a row of cameras mounted on their tripods like machine guns, flanked by tired men and women in button-up shirts with press accreditations around their necks or pinned to their blazers, juggling laptops and hand-held cameras. When it was over, I went back to the search bar and typed in Regan's name, but she wasn't there either.

32

It was the babies that were starting to really bother me: those sleeping or squalling bundles with the sun and rain kept off their heads by small arched umbrellas or frilled sunhats, their temperatures carefully regulated by their Spanish mothers, who spoke softly to them in the language of their patrimony. What did they do to deserve such intensive tuition? Look at them sleeping through it under the planes of Queen's Park: pink-cheeked, self-satisfied. They were being given key after key to the kingdom, keys they would neither grasp nor appreciate and which (the way the world was going) they might not even use, preferring the ubiquity of English, and keeping the other for their shadow lives. I wanted a shadow life too – I was tired of living in the open. At the rate my Spanish was growing, I could cast only minor shadows, the relief of a small boulder (*roca*) or a young bush (*arbusto*), when all the while I wanted a forest of ponderosa pine.

'What's wrong?' Nat asked. But he didn't want to know, he just wanted to be a cowboy. He went through a second rash of wanting nothing but pinto beans and mash, Tabasco sauce and corned beef, the trials of the harmonica, *All the Pretty Horses*. If I sat in the other room, I could pretend we were on separate sides of the Rio Grande, watching the stars the Aztecs used to read.

Still, he put on his dinner jacket from time to time, and didn't seem to mind the artifices of civilization when they came with good wine and chambers gossip, a chance to play his hand. So I found myself, now and then, in cocktail dress and heels, standing in a room that was empty except for the waiters with their backs to the bookshelves, the cellist tuning her instrument, and cocktail tables erupting like palm trees every few feet. On one particular evening – a retirement party for a lady barrister with an amateur interest in nineteenth-century science – the members of Nat's chambers were expected to arrive together. I walked slowly around the perimeter of the room, looking at the books on the shelves, which had titles like *Davy's Lamp* and *Michael Faraday: Citizen, Scientist, Seer*, and listened to the waiters talk. Was it noticeable, one said to the others, that he used a particularly Argentinian form of English? It couldn't be helped, he would always be from Argentina. No matter how much time he spent watching telly – he deployed the Anglicism with not a little pride – he couldn't get rid of his obviously Argentinian accent. 'I didn't know you were Argentinian,' the second waiter, an English girl, said flatly. The third waiter explained that his own accent was the product of Puglia. 'Puglia?' said the Argentinian. 'Puglia,' confirmed the third waiter. 'Can you imagine the standards of English in Puglia? I was a genius. I was the best in my class!'

'Have you ever thought about pushing one of the busts out the window?' said the girl. 'I mean, just walking over and shoving it out on to the street below.'

'They are locked,' said the Argentinian knowledgeably.

'I mean, wouldn't it make things interesting?' the girl said.

The other two waiters were either used to the girl or unexcitable by temperament because neither of them bothered to respond. I couldn't help looking out the window to see how many heads passed under me – three, three rich, unbroken heads. The cellist was above it all, rosining her bow, warming up her fingers, with her tuxedo and her velvet scrunchy and the glasses that took up half her face. I couldn't decide if she was very ugly or very cool. Was she fuckable? If Nat had been next to me, I would have asked him. We played a game sometimes when we were waiting, or tired of talking, in an airport or at a restaurant, when I invited him to rate the fuckability of women as they passed. Nat never followed women with his eyes – at least, not so I noticed. I had never seen him lose control of a sentence because a blonde crossed his line of vision. I'd been told I should be grateful to be spared this common humiliation, which gets more common as one ages, but the game taught me that practically every woman under the age of forty was fuckable, along with a few women over it. More specifically, I learned that Nat had an entirely conventional set of aesthetics – that he liked women in skirts, women who were thin but large breasted, that he was a man who could take the rough with the smooth, that, despite his family (or maybe because of it), vulgarity didn't turn him off, that caked-on make-up and fake tans did not detract from a good pair of legs – and that he had unexpected weaknesses: red hair, shoulder tattoos, flat chests on women with strong cheekbones and sharp jaws, women I had thought would end up looking like harpies. But he never rated their trajectory: he was seeing them now, this angle, this hour. In these moments, when he was assessing strangers and I

175

was providing means and motive, I became more like Nat's stepsister than his wife. Each woman we analyzed made us co-conspirators, not lovers. In the moment where my curiosity displaced any sexual jealousy, for the sake of the game, we became sexless ourselves. The game never went the other way. Nat never asked me how fuckable certain men were. He was hostile to any playful suggestion that the game's tables should turn. He had no curiosity about my private admirations, and I never insisted. Except for a few occasions, I'd never stared at someone on the Tube; never been tempted to follow someone over the Millennium Bridge. So why keep playing? The game was an exercise in training Nat's attention away from me, teaching him how to look and admire elsewhere, teaching myself to be immune to his mental absence. It was our most decadent pastime, our most common corruption.

He didn't see the cellist. I saw him walk into the library with a flock of partners, talking animatedly to a small woman in flats with smudged grey hair. He led her through the crowd over to me. 'Elspeth,' he said, 'this is my wife, Margit – Margit, this is our head of chambers, Elspeth Hunt.'

'Pleasure,' said Elspeth Hunt, a woman with the gift of producing a natural smile to order, a smile for an old friend met by chance after many years. 'Nat has told me so much about you,' she said. She turned to accept a glass of champagne from a waiter, the Argentinian. 'I'd like to read your work – it's in the *Independent*, isn't it? – but I can't seem to find time to read the newspapers, regardless of each year's resolutions.'

I looked at Nat; he looked steadily at Elspeth Hunt.

'Actually,' she continued, 'although we still buy newspapers – on principle – my youngest son recently showed me how to listen to podcasts, and the daily news podcasts are really quite good.' She laughed regretfully. 'Of course, they're all very well and good in one's home, but you get all sorts listening to them on their bicycles, don't you? On the Tube, and walking down the street? Collisions waiting to happen.'

Nat nodded with great understanding.

'My husband would say "Cases waiting to happen",' said the head of chambers, and I could tell from her delivery that this was Nat's line and he'd missed his cue.

'I shall stop before I become even more censorious,' said Elspeth Hunt. 'In fact, I see Sam Keppel standing near Darwin. He promised me a dirty joke and I'm going to take him up on it.' She smiled again, before turning to make her way through the increasingly crowded library.

'The *Independent*?' I said.

In the cracks of conversation, the cellist came through: a long plume of seventeenth-century sound, like a brass glint on a revolving orrery.

After a pause Nat said, 'Don't you know anyone who grew up in an army family?' Tailored suits manoeuvred around backless dresses. Hands clasped, cheeks kissed, shoulders squeezed. 'When they're asked where they're from, they'll say Salisbury, or Ohio, or Germany, even if they only spent nine months there. Some people deserve the whole story, sometimes it's better to have your Salisbury.' As he spoke, he looked around the room, taking its temperature, assessing where the dead spots were, where the laughter was coming from.

'Why not say I was an artist?' I said eventually.

'Please,' he said. 'They'd ask you where you got your weed. Besides, some of them would ask to see your work, to ask how much it is. Nobody reads the *Independent*; they all like to think of themselves as patrons.'

Will approached in a blue suit, a shade too dandyish for navy, with a floral pocket handkerchief.

'Where's Irma?' I said, raising my voice as the voices in the library intensified.

Irma was at the hospital, Will said. Her father had returned from Mexico and had forgotten which side of the road he was supposed to drive on. 'It's not serious,' he assured us. 'He sprained his neck, but he didn't break anything. He didn't suffer any kind of concussion. But her mother's hysterical, she turns anything into a drama. Irma is one of the only people who can calm her down.' I heard a bruise of disapproval in his tone, a slight – or not so slight – exasperation at such amateur manipulation.

'And how go the bodies?' Will asked me, just as a short, plump arm, constrained by the narrowness of its jacket, reached apologetically between us for a speared olive. 'Bodies?' the owner of the arm said, eyebrows raised. 'Sorry, none of my business, none of my business.' But instead of retreating, the man turned his round, boy-emperor face to me. 'You're in medicine, are you?' he said. 'None of my business, of course.'

'I'm a journalist,' I said. 'Mexico.' It came easily now; it was just a tag around my neck.

'A correspondent, are you?' the man said, speaking in a skimming, vicarish voice. 'You belong to the Frontline?' he said, and extended his hand. 'Richard Bowles, clinical negligence. Rather old-fashioned, the Frontline,' he said, when all hands were shaken. 'My nephew's a member. Bloody fantastic rib-eye, though, if you'll pardon my French.'

When I said I only went there for drinks, he shuddered.

'Oh no no no,' said Richard Bowles. 'You have to eat the

rib-eye. I insist. Next time, order dinner, you won't regret it.' As he spoke, I couldn't help looking above the rise of his belly at a button hole that gaped each time he breathed, showing a pinch of ruddy skin from which black wiry hairs rose and intercoiled. He reached his hand out for his flute. 'Crumbs,' he said. 'I could have sworn I put my drink right here.' With that, he wandered off.

In the wake of Richard Bowles, the waiter from Puglia topped us up. The champagne evaporated into bubbles which floated up to the ivory cornices of the library ceiling. Nearer the earth, women wore their hair buttery and full, curling at the shoulders, or combed back carefully into knots and buns: hair which aimed to master that impossible compromise between femininity and power. Liv was there too, her yellow hair in its apprenticeship. She joined us on her second glass. 'This has gone straight to my head,' she said, after kissing us one by one. 'I'm standing with you so I don't make a fool of myself in front of one of the QCs.'

'I think that's technically your brief for the evening,' said Will.

She was used to having them on her own, her boys. She was used to the casual, teasing tone one woman uses to address several men, and which they use with her in return, the presence of another woman making it sound artificial, camp.

'Nat says you're working on something really big,' Liv said, with ripe, sisterly camaraderie. 'When you're finished you must send it to me. The link, I mean.'

'It'll be a while,' I said, watching Nat walk away to find the waiter from Puglia, Will at his elbow.

'But how exciting to have such a big *project*,' she said. 'I imagine that you have a whole wall covered with pictures and string, you know, like the detectives have in the movies. What do they call it? An evidence board? Does that sound right?'

She wasn't pretty exactly, Liv – her mouth was too heavy, or something. But she had an aura of sexual frankness. She was the sort of person who knew how dating apps worked; used them when she must without self-consciousness. She'd never complain that she wished the Internet didn't exist: that life was better when people met in lifts and in bars. She still met men in bars and in lifts. She had accepted the cost of a Brazilian every two weeks. She paid for it as one paid for the Internet, as an acceptable tax on living.

It was already the time of the evening when the first drink had been spilled and passed off as clumsiness. Walking through the library was like being trapped in a market scene in a big-budget historical film just before a public execution. Everywhere I went I heard words like 'seconded' and 'ombudsman' and 'revocation'. Also, 'IGAs' and 'percentages', and even 'Philip Roth'. If there were judges present, they didn't look any different from the others. They watched their weight, dyed their roots, went to the theatre and holidayed in France like everybody else. Nat was standing in the corner of the room with a slender white-haired, bearded man with a sceptical knot of eyebrows, a man with whom, judging by their posture, he was exchanging confidential information. That's when I saw that we'd run out of time. I had thought it would be a year or two at least before the convergence. All Nat's nagging uncertainties, his doubts, his private insecurities about his value to chambers, those conversations from the day before that he replayed to shake out all their possible meanings like crumbs from a napkin, all of this had kept him himself. But he was losing his uncertainty, losing all doubt, growing deaf to second and third interpretations when they disturbed his dinner, standing confidently among his colleagues, with equal solvency and ambitions never wholly sedated, becoming more and more like this species, and leaving the race we had formed together, the clan of two, to the evolutionary past.

I drained my flute and, as I left the room, I felt like running my fingers over the wall, which is how I knew I'd had too much to drink. I took my time on the stairs, pretending to type into my phone, to see whether Nat would notice now, or now, or now, that I'd gone. But the end of the night was already played out. I went down the stairs and out the doors on to Albemarle Street. There was a coat missing. I was missing my coat. I went back into the Royal Institution and the cloakroom attendant said nothing about my wet face or my clamped voice. He didn't say, Are you okay? He was thinking, It's that time of the evening again: the hour of weeping women. Silly bitch, he was thinking, after all that free champagne.

Outside again on Albemarle Street, I walked several steps in the direction of Piccadilly and then sat on the scoured steps of a jeweller's, locked up for the evening, the empty velvet pedestals framed by tasselled curtains in the window. The clamp was still on my throat. I wished it would spread to my face. I waited for someone to stop and ask me if I needed help, but no one stopped. Men and women passed in attitudes of polite inattention. I wanted Nat to come out to me, to wander past me and then look up, to be stopped in his tracks by my misery. To cross-examine me kindly, to help me come to the bottom of it, this wetness. Or would he just say, 'You've had too much to drink,' an observation that would come to haunt me at every future party, whenever I reached for another glass and he said, 'Darling' in the way that meant, 'Do you remember what a catastrophe you were last time?'

That got me on my feet. Walking again past the houses of high fashion, the arcades and the cocktail bars of Albemarle Street, until I reached Piccadilly in fully electrified Friday force: music at cross purposes, busking trumpeters and passing car radios, the clock at Fortnum & Mason, the last hour of entry at the Royal Academy. I could cry in Mexico City, I thought. I could sit on a set of stairs, or lean against a building, and cry. I could have a cigarette in my hand, but I wouldn't need one. No one would look past me in polite embarrassment. They would think: it's the hour for weeping women. They have to do it somehow, why not now in the company of strangers? In this case, the case of the weeping women, the sisterhood of women with broken hearts, or momentary lapses, or sudden memories, or just the desire to get something off their chests, Mexico promised a safe haven. I was sure I could go to Mexico City right now and find a niche, a bench near a park, or outside a church, a chair in a library, or in a bar with a mezzanine, and use up the rest of my tears. I'd feel at home, or at least I'd feel the consolation of being in the right place, like a sinner in a confessional box. Now, here, on Piccadilly, standing beside restaurants whose windows were crowded with plates of oysters, watching men in suits argue over who would carry the first round, over which wallet would be first in hand, watching the Ritz across the road wink and glitter, I felt the way a dog feels when it's given its new family the slip and tries to find its way back to its mother, only to run into the hard world of thieves and dogcatchers. But perhaps London was more like Mexico City than it knew, because in London, too, people could go missing. In London, they fell silent, faded, until it was no longer possible to see them coming or going. It wouldn't be too hard, I thought, to see the signs starting to show on the surface of your skin.

33

As much as I hated taking a hint from Liv, whose conversations with Nat always seemed too knowing, even complicit (there was always an air of oral sex about Liv), it had not occurred to me to make an evidence board. I associated them with men at the end of their tether, but there was no need for me to get on a high horse, I thought, since either way they surely belonged to the same category as maps and diagrams.

So, after a rough shift at the clinic, where I later heard that a patient had wept quietly throughout her procedure, the liquid border of that city of weeping women perpetually expanding, I spread my haul – a large cork bulletin board, pins, permanent markers, string and the photographs I had printed on Kilburn High Road – over the coffee table. I had chosen a picture of the mayor and his wife taken before the fall, an image of an attractive couple wearing expressions of seriousness that couldn't quite efface their bloom. I'd expected a witchy-looking woman with a long nose (Pineda Villa – pins – pine needles) and a lumpy older man in an ill-fitting suit. Instead, I saw a couple who carried a radiance with them, a glow of tennis-court health, the confidence of people who had been lucky and who had no reason not to expect their luck to continue. Later photographs, after their arrest, after months of detention, showed that Abarca had aged twenty years, his cheeks sunken, his eyes wary; his wife appeared without her signature smoky eyeliner, her hair unwashed and pulled away from her face. They had become just another couple brought low by disaster, shattered like any other husband and wife who'd had their lives foreclosed.

In addition to the photographs of Abarca and Pineda Villa, I had one of the President, Enrique Peña Nieto, waving smugly from his podium, and one of the Attorney General, Murillo Karam, who looked even more like a Vichy chief of police. There was a photograph of the bullet-riddled buses at Juan N. Alvarez and Periférico Norte, and there were photographs of the forensic team at the Cocula dump and at the riverside where the black bags containing the remains of Alexander Mora Venancio were discovered, or, rather, where they had been forged. I had a photograph of the morose, bulldog-jowled Felipe Flores Velázquez, the chief of police in Iguala, and I would have liked to have had another of Captain José Martínez Crespo, one of the commanders of the 27th Infantry Battalion, but he was harder to find. There was the printout of the government's poster of the missing students, but the images of their faces were grainy and the names printed below unclear.

The problem that faced me was the relationship between the photographs. What would the significance be of their positions, the distances between them, the preference of one image over another, the decision to pin a certain photograph above or below? In order to calibrate the relations between the photographs correctly, I would have to already know those relations, at which point the evidence board wouldn't be so much a tool as a memorandum. Since I had no proof of these relations, since relations were in fact highly disputed, secret, even (in a manner of speaking) forged, it was imperative, I thought, to take an intentionally naïve approach. I took the photographs out of the envelope they had arrived in and placed them face down on the carpet. In this way, they were indistinguishable from each other, printed as they were on identical card stock of the same length and width, although it would have made more sense to enlarge certain images, such as the reproduction of the government's poster of the missing forty-three, for example, a copy of which I had left in Mother Pacifica's flat.

Once the photographs were spread out, I began to move them gradually across the carpet, pushing them in wide, vague orbits. I moved the overturned photographs gingerly, like an apprentice croupier: I plaited them in invisible braids, making figures of eight the way children move hot sand with their feet in search of cooler layers beneath, or as inexperienced card players shuffle their decks. When I could no longer predict the image on their reverse, when I couldn't even begin to guess which image each photograph was keeping to itself, I collected them into a pile and laid them out, photograph by photograph, across the bulletin board, like a tarot spread. On the first shuffle, the row of photographs looked like coffins awaiting mass burial. From left to right I turned over the Attorney General, Jesús Murillo Karam; the chief of the Iguala police, Felipe Flores Velásquez; President Enrique Peña Nieto; and the miniature faces of the missing forty-three from my poor reproduction. On the second row: the former mayor, José Luis Abarca Velázquez, and his wife, María de los Ángeles Pineda Villa; the bullet-riddled buses; the forensic team.

On the second shuffle, I grew bolder, placing a photograph at the centre of the board (the one of the students), and one in each of the four corners (top left: the chief of police, Felipe Flores Velásquez; top right: the Attorney General, Jesús Murillo Karam; bottom right: the former mayor, José Luis Abarca, and his wife, María de los Ángeles Pineda Villa; bottom left: the bullet-riddled buses), with a photograph at the very top, of President Enrique Peña Nieto grinning benevolently from an elevated post, like a bearded god on an old map, presiding over all below.

Then I saw that the position of the photographs was only my first challenge. I'd thought the ball of string I'd bought might make the relation between the photographs more expressive, particularly the relation between the photographs at a greater distance from each other. The string would create a looser, more tangential form of connection: more easily revised than the photographs, it would allow for more flexible enquiry, for the intuition, experimentation and openness González Rodríguez insisted was necessary for a successful investigation. Once I began to unwind the string, however, I tripped over the problem of direction and causation. Who could say what the connection between the photographs that was represented by the line of string meant? Who was to say whether the connection travelled in one direction, like a neuron, or in circles, like an electric circuit? Just as the camera had traversed that poor weeping woman's colon earlier in the day, registering each curve and obstruction, so, in the bowels of the crime, my eye followed each ravel and kink of the string.

When Nat came home from his run, his sweat leaving extravagant Rorschach blots on his shirt, he found me still fumbling at the coffee table. 'Arts and crafts?' he said, leaning over me, filling the room with the smell of stale sweat. There was a time the smell of his sweat made me think about sex. It was the smell of stiff rumpled sheets, hot skin, quick breaths; and, in the streets of Barcelona down below, it smelled like the promise of shade, and the sound of hawkers, horns, children, tourists, dogs. Just then I felt the tug of another string, a ripple along an inner thread quivering from one point to the next. Without turning away from the board, I reached behind me and put my hand on Nat's damp calf. I slid it up the narrow curve of his leg, over the hardness of his bones. When I reached his thigh, he stood up and stepped back.

He took another step backwards and collapsed on the couch, for which he was a foot too long, and lay still for a long moment. 'You know what you need?' he said, struggling to sit up. When he'd come home the night before, hours after I did, he had said nothing about my disappearance from the party. It was as if he were adopting an attitude of mature, even parental inattention, an intentional, silently corrective blindness. The cruellest thing about Nat was how he could retract himself, climb into bed and fall asleep within minutes.

'What do I need?' I said, returning to the board and considering the metaphysical question of whether perhaps the map and not the victims ought to be at the centre.

Without answering his own question, Nat went into the bathroom. After a minute the spatter of the shower came on, tentative and then full throttle. From the sound of the spurt, I could hear that the shower curtain had not wholly closed, that the water was refracting against all the surfaces, the tiled walls and the curtain, and especially the bathroom floor, which, when Nat stepped out, would be swamped, the bath mat a dark island slowly going to mould. When he came out again, he stood in the hallway with his towel. 'Is this' – he gestured to the board in a wide sweep – 'because of your dad?' As he talked, he began to dry his body, rubbing himself fiercely on the upper side of his narrow thigh, on the underside of his haunch. 'Is this supposed to compensate you for some childhood trauma? Because I don't know how else to make sense of it.' All of his body was long and spare and covered with fine gold wires.

'You don't have to make anything of it,' I said, getting to my feet. What is this obsession with origins? I thought. Why does everything have to come from somewhere? Why can't it be born fully grown, straight from the forehead?

That's when I saw from the look on Nat's face, from his fumbling with the towel, that he had an investigation of his own, that he was investigating the disappearance of desire. He had discovered that there were other forms of disappearing in plain sight than the kind that happened in Guerrero. That no one pays attention when the tracks are covered over, or covered up, or when the ground is eroded by the rain that falls overnight.

'It has nothing to do with you,' I said, turning back to the board and gathering up its elements.

'Of course it has to do with me,' Nat said, tying his towel around his waist. He was a terrible detective, I saw. He had only been taught one kind of questioning. He asked questions which presupposed their answers, questions which drove at the answers they already knew, like hammers on nails. But his were hammers that only worked when the nails were straight and stayed straight all the way down. He had never been taught the art of the open question: the question that conceals no trap, the naïve question, the credulous – even ignorant – question. He had nothing to do with nails that bent under their own weight, nails that became skewed by use or by nature, and which had to be dealt with at an angle: nails that could only be tackled by a mind that itself could bend, could coil in and double back, a mind made for a labyrinth, for the spider's web, for the thread running through.

When he asked if I'd leave him alone, go out for the day, it was one more question he already knew the answer to.

34

Besides the Mare, which I was saving for last, there was one place I hadn't checked for Regan. I took the Tube to Walthamstow: an inefficient journey, a tangle of lines. Between Baker Street and Oxford Circus, I sat very still and checked myself for punctures. It had taken a while for Nat to express his anger: months of his tightened mouth, rigid posture and strangled kisses. Even after our first fight – an argument which began after I used a metal spatula on his saucepan, and which quickly disintegrated into his accusing me of an overall disregard for things (as was clear, he said, from my possessions' general degradation, their tendency to break down) – he had been slow to anger. He preferred to change the subject, or to leave the room and come back with a cooler head. There are people who become more articulate under the pressure of their anger and those who become mute. You'd think that, as a barrister, Nat would be in the first category, but no: in court, he confided after an argument, his advantage was his temperament, his ability to ignore small-mindedness and continue evenly and logically.

Why hadn't I taken the overground train from West Hampstead to Blackhorse Road? I wondered. It was an hour and a half before I stood in front of 17 Tandey Street, one of an optimistic row of modest terraced houses, bright with the charm of being newly bought: flowers and kitchen herbs on the windowsills of the upper storeys, the grass of the postage-stamp-sized front gardens freshly cut. When I rang Martha's doorbell, it had just gone six o'clock.

When the door opened, there she was, wearing a faded mint-coloured apron with an aroma of meat behind her. I had remembered Regan's ex-girlfriend as tired and grey-haired, but now I saw her hair was silvery blonde, not grey, longer than it was when I saw her last, long enough for her to braid it around her head like a Scandinavian farmer's wife. Women who wore their hair like Martha's looked like they had just been told they were mothers, and had decided to keep the news to themselves, a fierce, private joy.

'Hello Margit,' she said. Martha's great gift was never to show surprise.

'Can I come in for a few minutes?' I asked.

After a pause, she opened the door wider. 'You can't stay long, I'm afraid,' she said, and turned away to walk back to her kitchen, leaving me to close the door. 'I'm expecting friends.'

The wooden floors had been recently swept: shoes were lined up on the stairs with the forlorn hope of orphans, waiting to be chosen. Flowers waited in a glass vase on the dining table, big orange trumpets, and leafy plants in various shades of green sprouted and trailed from painted ceramic pots in the corners of the rooms we walked through. I saw no obvious signs of loneliness: no cat, no half-covered keyboard. The kitchen was painted an expensive primrose yellow, and, on the wall, a calendar of vintage travel posters was turned to the right month. Flour streaked the wooden worktop, and scraps of papery garlic skin and onion ends and carrot shavings had been pushed into a mottled mound. The radio was on, voices woven into a carpet of crisp consonants and wry vowels.

'Have you been here before?' she asked, taking a pint of double cream from the fridge. In fact, I had seen the house before: a year or two ago, when Regan invited us to a dinner party. She had bragged about Martha's cooking skills, had talked terrines and truffles, cotton napkins and cheroots. When we arrived, the house was pulsating with people: drinkers in the kitchen, smokers in the garden. The dining table was covered in paper plates and takeaway containers – Szechuan, Keralan, Nepalese – and the deliciously greasy air was starting to stale. Martha had hardly moved from the armchair in which she had taken up residence, watching the evening pass. 'She said it was my party,' Regan told us later. 'When she found out how many people I'd invited, she said, *You* do it. I was like – *I* can't fucking cook. I burn fish fingers.'

I had disliked Martha then, and her oyster-like way of sitting in her chair. She had seemed like a woman with no give. But seeing her now, in her apron and her bare feet, with her braided coronet, pouring double cream into a bowl and taking up her whisk, I wondered if it had been her way of refusing to join the circus without forbidding the circus its existence; a way of maintaining her preferences without denying Regan's. Still, everyone knew she wasn't happy in the armchair: her mouth had soured, as if she'd had too much gin.

Now, red wine in a cut glass waited on the worktop, next to a cookbook with its pages clipped open with clothes pegs.

There was no sign of the bottle other than the glass. If she offered, I decided, I wouldn't say no. But she didn't offer. She neither acknowledged the half-drunk glass nor picked it up. I began to think that she'd stopped drinking in order to spare herself the obligation of making a reluctant invitation. The longer I stayed in Martha's house, the more I wanted a glass of her red wine. Would it be so hard for her to ask me what I was doing, to say in a rush of generosity, 'Add another plate to the table'? But despite every sign of life about her, her flowers and her bloom, Martha was still Martha: still inflexible, still iron-fisted, Empress of Russia. In her mind there were never too many open windows. The scraps of food on her work-top were a concession. All those pretty things – the orange flowers, the books on the shelves, the primrose walls – were signs of her inability to make do with the wrong props. Then I thought, I'd never know Martha without Regan's inter-ference. I was always her friend first.

'Did you have anything particular you wanted to say?' Martha said, walking as she whisked, holding the bowl under the crook of her left arm against her hip, as though taking a restless baby for a stroll.

At Regan's party, she had sat in the armchair, thinking unthinkable thoughts, sipping gin from one of her great-aunt's green wine glasses. Regan, who hated those green glasses, had planned and schemed, had handed them to irresponsible friends, but they never did break. They were in Martha's kitchen still, high on a wooden shelf, next to the umber pyramid of the tagine dish. All at once it felt cata-strophic for me to be there, in Martha's house, before her dinner party; catastrophic to have taken the Tube to Wal-thamstow in search of a friend who didn't want to be found.

I was the papery garlic skins, the carrots' bearded nubs and the barren stems of thyme: unwanted proof of what had happened.

'It's about Regan,' I said.

Martha looked at me as if to say, *No shit.* 'You know we're not together,' she said.

'I know, Regan said. But I wondered if you knew where she was.'

She was whisking faster now, her wrist taking all that the cream could throw. 'Do you know why we're no longer together?' she asked. After a pause she added, 'I'll save you the trouble of guessing by saying it's not because we couldn't agree on whether or not we wanted children.'

The whisk was scraping the bowl now and making thin tinny scratches, like a shell on a pane of glass.

'Regan is a teenager,' Martha said. 'She has all of a teenager's best qualities. She's spontaneous and magnetic and frustrating and clever and funny. She has a terrible attention span. She's charmed by her own mistakes. She flirts with anyone!' Martha set the bowl down and snapped off the radio. 'I mean, anyone: waitresses and baristas and police officers and drunks. DJs who say they have fatal illnesses, ridiculous people, fantasists, dramatists. When she doesn't come home at the end of the night, she says: journalism.' Martha paused, like someone stepping from a train on to the platform across a void that was wider than she'd expected. 'She was unfaithful once, you know, soon after we first got together.'

Was I surprised? Not at this news about Regan, the brigand, but I was surprised that Martha with her tenacious privacy had let it out. She scraped the whipped cream into a Denby bowl and, covering it with a small plate, slotted it into one of the clear shelves of her enormous two-door American fridge.

'When someone is unfaithful to you at the beginning of a relationship,' Martha said, 'you know what to expect. Not right away, perhaps, there's too much remorse for that. And infidelity can be exhilarating, in its own way. The cheater enjoys the discomfort of waiting to be forgiven, of being punished. The wronged party enjoys withholding her affection, imposing penance, revising the terms of their contract.'

She began to pull out of the fridge pears, plums, apples, a repurposed ice-cream box brimming with blackberries. The fruit sat guiltily on the worktop while she found a paring knife.

'For some couples, one or both of them will invent crises to rediscover the emotional intensity that follows an infidelity. I only work with children, you know, but I rather like Adam Phillips's definition of a couple as two criminals in search of a crime.'

As she talked, she cut a plum into two, hooked her finger around the stone and pulled. She went on to tear stones out of each plum, the way the heart might be torn out of a sacrificial victim, viciously, superstitiously, with increasing exhilaration. 'After a few months pass,' continued Martha, 'after a year or so, when the exhilaration wears off, and the cheater is visibly restless, the wronged party remembers the beginning of the crisis, and starts looking for signs of bad faith. In short,' said Martha, 'it didn't end well.'

Still, you couldn't pity Martha, not with her pulpy, plum-covered hands, her green glasses and her orange flowers and her yellow kitchen. A harp's glissando zipped up and down from her phone: the sign that we should wake from the dream, that real life was reassembling itself around us.

Martha left her massacred plums and squatted in front of her oven. When she opened its door, the wet, rich smell of roasting meat made my stomach quiver. 'Ten minutes,' she said, with that old Martha frown.

'So you don't know where she is,' I said, while she cored and chopped the apples, the pears.

'Bingo,' said Martha.

'And you don't know where she could be?'

'She could be anywhere,' said Martha acidly, 'with any tramp, part-time model, failed comedian. Hopping from one flat to the next, anything to avoid signing a lease. Oh for God's sake,' she said, looking at me. 'You're not pining for her, are you?'

'You were at my wedding!' I said.

'Stop trying to contact her,' said Martha. 'Stop trying to catch her. Throw a party. Invite everyone. She might come. If she's in London, she'll come. I expect if she's in the Home Counties she'll come. She likes crowds.'

'Will you come? If I throw a party.'

'You mean, will I be your lure?' she said, and looked at her watch. 'I'm too old for this, Margit, and I'm afraid you'll have to go. My friends are coming any minute and I've got to roast hazelnuts. If I think about Regan and roast hazelnuts, they'll burn and taste like hell.'

When I reached the front step, Martha said, 'You can tell her I'm coming.'

'But *will* you come?' I asked again.

Through the closed door, I heard the weight and squeak of her bare feet retreating on the clean wooden floorboards to her primrose-coloured kitchen.

35

A dinner party, a fancy-dress party, a cocktail party, a garden party, a surprise party, a silent disco, a dawn rave, a masquerade, a midnight feast, a saint's day bash, a Halloween party, a Christmas-in-October party, a late autumn equinox party, an early winter solstice party, an early Bonfire Night party, a delayed German Unity Day party, a second anniversary party, a two-years-late housewarming party, a tea party, a street party, a buffet party, a bank holiday barbecue, a house party, a 'keg party', a pyjama party, a full moon party, a Nuit Blanche, an after-party.

36

But after what? The idea of a party was still tapping against my mind like a little golden mallet when the invitation to Patty Bercow's private view arrived in the mail. Patty! I thought when I opened it. Good old Patty from the Tate with the paint under her nails. Patty who hated Picasso without a qualm. 'How can you hate Picasso?' I had asked her on one of our lunch breaks as we sat on the South Bank of the Thames, looking at St Paul's. I was in the clutches of his Blue Period, and was thrilled by *La Celestina*'s dead, glaucomic eye.

Patty's finances had been precarious ever since I'd met her. She'd never bothered to hide the exorbitant expense of the divorce, both in psychological and financial terms, or her haphazard and overlapping part-time engagements which, she told us, gave her time for her art. Still, the invitation had been printed with no expense spared. The title of the show, *Patchwork*, appeared beneath a high-quality colour reproduction of what I supposed must be one of Patty's paintings: a large canvas covered in cross-hatched shades of blue and grey which, if you looked at it out of the corner of your eye, might be a seascape. It was the kind of painting whose brushstrokes would be called confrontational if it had been produced by a famous painter, and incoherent if it was painted by an unknown artist. A single thread of orange travelled along one of the thick blue undulations. It was a terrible title, I thought: homely and self-effacing. It suggested sewing bees and quilting circles, women in wagons mending the knees of their husbands' trousers and the elbows of their shirts. Not even Eva Hesse or Louise Bourgeois could make me rethink how I felt about textiles, or get rid of that smell of second best. I decided to go in spite of the title: not least because I wanted to get out of the house. Nat's campaign of politeness, his well-bred way of skirting around me in the kitchen and not looking me in the eye when I spoke was getting on my nerves.

Patty's show was held at a small gallery on a quiet Georgian street in Borough. Tucked into the brickwork on the far side of an underpass over which the train tracks ran, the gallery looked like the former premises of a nineteenth-century firm where desks of penniless and disappointed clerks had once stood in relentless rows. The thing was to be cheerful, I thought. Hearty and congratulatory. The point is that you *did* it, I'd say to Patty as we looked around an empty room.

But as I approached the gallery, I could feel its pulse. From the street I heard a hive of voices coming from behind its front door, a hum smeared as if heard underwater. For a minute, instead of opening the door and going inside, I stood on the street looking through the windows. A party, I thought: a party, a party. Not a mallet now, but a golden Swiss clock, chiming on the hour.

Inside, plunging in past the pram left in the doorway, and pushing through a crowd of trench coats and wool cardigans, I caught sight of Patty. 'You came!' she said, when the man with Warhol hair and expensive spectacles had moved on.

She put a warm hand on my arm, which was the closest Patty came to giving a hug. I made a face at her and a gesture that took in the room and said *Wow. Look at this! Look at you!* but Patty gave no sign of shared surprise or pleasure or embarrassment or flattery. She was like a cashier waiting at the till of a shop attached to a petrol station. The work had a separate life now, she seemed to suggest, looking at her paintings as coolly as if they were nothing more than teeth that had been pulled out and laid on a paper towel.

'Let's get you a drink,' Patty said, and she began to move across the room in that particular way of hers that I'd forgotten: that old stiff walk which seemed to try to avoid a tenderness in her hip. It was a walk on the verge of a hobble, a walk that suggested she'd suffered a childhood injury and, despite all the operations and the physiotherapy, had never quite regained her earlier freedom of movement. That rigid walk of hers gave her the look of a peasant woman, an impression she encouraged through the dark smocks she'd worn for years over a pair of dark tights, refusing to show her legs or her shoulders or her arms. It was as if she'd decided that the time for such revelations was over, or perhaps it was because of some secret dislike – of thick dark hair on her forearms, say, or a rash or scar she could no longer be bothered to explain.

The gallery was no more than a single room with several shallow recesses, but it took determination to reach the table at which a boy and girl relentlessly poured out bottles of Prosecco into cheap wine glasses. Patty handed one back to me and waved away the glass the boy held out to her. 'Young people!' she said, and she introduced me to Ben and Amy, who worked part-time or volunteered (it was too loud for specifics) at the gallery in which we were standing. From their blank faces, I thought they couldn't have been more than twenty or twenty-one, living in Dalston in a house share where they paid almost nothing in rent, but where the bath was constantly threatening to fall through the floor. When Patty was drawn to one side by a woman in a red beret, Ben and Amy asked me how I knew her. They'd taken a few of her classes, they said. She was an excellent teacher. She took them seriously. In their experience, with their backgrounds, very few people took them seriously, they said. 'There's something maternal about her,' said Ben. 'What?' he said when Amy rolled her eyes. 'There *is*. I want her to mother me.'

Did Patty have children? I wondered, looking around to see if I could catch a family resemblance in the crowd: some iteration of her Armenian nose or talkative hands. You'd think it would have come up when she talked about her divorce. If she'd had children, surely she would have mentioned nursery or school fees or co-parenting with her bastard of an ex. Then again, clearly, she was a woman whose inner coastline hid secluded sea caves. She liked the idea of pathways cut off by the tide, she liked the idea of the private beach, the drowned grotto, the stone steps that lead down the sheer edge. Otherwise, we'd have had some idea of her work, of its growing significance. We'd have known that it would lead to this. Years ago, when she and I took our lunch breaks together and sat on the South Bank eating slices of café quiche, Patty didn't mind talking about her projects. She described them matter-of-factly: art was just a question of time, space and money. And since discussions of her work were without anxiety, without any reference to the imagination, or inspiration, or influences, I'd had the impression that she wasn't very good. Or rather that being good wasn't as important as following the footpaths of her own inclination – the freedom to make bad art, if that's what she liked. Because I'd thought her work couldn't be very good, I'd never asked to see photographs. I'd imagined her making watercolours of seaside towns, or cottages in rural hamlets, cartoonishly round women embracing grandchildren or geese, or pictures of flowers, ferns and other sentimental shapes.

Across the room, I caught sight of the painting that had been printed on the invitation I'd received in the post. It was large, unexpectedly large, and when I looked at it closely I could see what I'd missed in the reproduction, that the darker patches of blue and grey were not thickened brushstrokes but thread – stitched over the paint, sudden textured density, neatly done although it must have taken force to get the needle through without damaging the paint.

The gallery was dense enough for private conversations to become public property. One man, with a ring of white hair consoling his bald crown, thought the paintings might be homages to Dubuffet's landscapes of Algeria, which he'd seen in Belgium. His companion, not to be outdone, wondered where the artist bought her thread, which he described as both robust and tender. Behind them, ignoring the art altogether, two graduate students debated the translation of 'patchwork' into French, German and Italian. 'It's *le patchwork*,' one insisted, to the other's indignation. Each time a painting sold, one of the assistants, either Ben or Amy, placed a yellow dot over the price. None of the prices Patty asked for her work were unreasonable or extravagant as far as art went, but they would add up quickly, given the proliferation of yellow dots across the room, dots which appeared beside the larger works as well as the smaller, more modestly priced pieces, those just within reach for patrons on tighter budgets, who snapped them up just as fiercely as their wealthier rivals did their more expensive neighbours. I thought I caught a glimpse of Marcello Greave's old assistant, Imogen, taking notes on the back of a postcard. Meanwhile, admirers stopped Patty to tell her how *immense* her work was, how *vertiginous*, and she thanked them as if they'd complimented her on the loveliness of a friend's garden she'd been watering while the owner was away. When a German in a quilted coat asked her where she got her inspiration from, whether the paintings were representations of landscapes she had known at a form-ative period – her childhood, perhaps? – Patty said, 'They're not representations of anything.' Given the titles of the paint-ings – *Within Sight of the Cape, Hinterlands, (Not) Crossing the Border* – I thought this was disingenuous, unless she was speaking literally: that her paintings didn't represent places, that they *were* those places, even if only in an emotional sense. But she wouldn't be drawn on what the pictures meant.

'Meanings don't interest me,' Patty said, and it was from the way she spoke – without self-consciousness or evasion, with a peasant's diffidence and a peasant's lack of curios-ity – that I saw how serious she was. She had no interest in convincing people of her paintings' value. They could look or not look. They could like or not like. When a man with a reporter's notepad stopped Patty to ask how she worked, she described her process of diluting various layers of paint with walnut oil, and the importance of making her stitches before the paint dried. But her description had more in common with a surgeon's account of the procedure he'd just carried out, or with a mechanic describing his replacement of part of an engine, than with anything else.

Where had she *come* from? I thought, standing in front of another large canvas, which seemed to depict a sandpit or a quarry, painted in rough strokes of yellow and white, with patches of embroidered brown, and the odd thread of silver and scarlet streaked across, a seam of ore to throw the eye. Was it a sandpit or a beach? I wondered. Was it an escarp-ment or a close-grained image of an ageing head of blonde hair? Was it a blurred field of wheat or a nauseatingly close look at a camelhair coat? Despite my training, despite all the permission I'd been taught to give modern art to be free of meaning, to be free of intention, to please the eye or frustrate it, to give it the middle finger, I felt a sudden, intense and agitated desire for an explanation. What was she playing at? I thought. Patty's poise, her new and established artist persona, the work she'd painted and patched in secret. There was something devious in all of this, I thought, with her pretending to be ordinary while she was carrying the work inside her. Something uncanny in the way she was exhibiting it without apparently second-guessing herself or defending herself against those whom it rubbed the wrong way.

There were two kinds of women, I thought: two kinds who stood in the way of disaster. Some of them were hit on the head, like Lady Lucan, and the others took their husbands to court, stayed sober, refused the money (up to a point) and made art. Then I thought, for the first time, although it should have struck me long before, that the strange thing about the missing forty-three students was that none of them were women. That in a country of missing and murdered women, as both Roberto Bolaño and Sergio González Rodríguez had documented, only men had disappeared on the night of 26 September. Then I thought: maybe the reason I hadn't made any inroads into the disappearance of the forty-three was because I was a woman. Maybe women should investigate the deaths and disappearances of women, and men should solve the crimes of men. Women might be better able to think like other women, and find the clues left by female victims to solve the crimes that were being done to them, whereas men were another question altogether. But who would investigate crimes against children? I thought. Anyway, most crimes were committed by men. And from there the line of argument quickly unravelled. I had the feeling that the painting in front of me was egging me on, somehow, making me more and more incoherent, like Patty's brushstrokes. The longer I looked at the painting, the more savage it became. It was like the hunting grounds of the chupacabra, the desert vampire that leaves nothing but carcasses and conjecture in its wake, casting hairless shadows against the henhouse, or glimpses of slick, moon-coloured skin. The dark patches of Patty's stitchwork across the canvas were bruises, or the bodies of small animals, evidence of some altercation. I wondered if she'd found a clever way to cover up her mistakes: if she'd hidden them under our very noses all along.

37

The next morning, the queasy, hungover feeling I'd had after the Oxford and Cambridge Club was back. I nursed it on the Jubilee line while the shrieking wheels raked the tracks. When the sound of the train fell away, we sat in the carriage like fishing boats in a harbour after the storm, feeling the waves lap against our hulls. In my uneasy state, I felt the full absurdity of the other passengers – the man sleeping against the window despite the jostling of his head, the student pretending to read *War and Peace*, the businesswoman tentatively tonguing an apple, as though she suspected that at any moment she'd lose a tooth. They were so complacent, so unchanged by their journey, and all the while this pit waited beneath me. Was it time, then, to give up? Was it time to put away the notebook, to close the tabs, to delete the links I'd archived, to leave my dog-eared library at the roadside, to unpin the photographs from my board and unwind the string that joined them, to weed out the phrases of Spanish just now beginning to take root?

The queasiness, the feeling of lead, would not lift. The previous night, I'd heard Patty say to another artist, a sculptor, that she knew she was going to make a big painting because she felt it in her intestines, a shiver of unfinished business. She had always been comfortable talking about her body. The other gallery assistants and I thought that was what happened when you were in your forties, and became increasingly physically feral. She knew she would paint something substantial, Patty said to the sculptor, from the weight in her gut and, at the same time, from her sense of accumulating liquid, a sense of something about to spill over. Which was not to say that when the work was finished, she would feel a release. The idea of release was bullshit, as far as Patty was concerned, although she could only speak for herself, she said, giving the sculptor an opening to disagree.

Forgeries, too, could be felt in the body, or so I'd read. Or rather, from time to time a detective or authenticator discovered a forgery through a lack of feeling, the absence of the prickle of recognition you expected to see when looking at an old master. So many bodies on constant alert, I thought, and I wondered if investigators, detectives and journalists, were statistically more likely to die of certain diseases such as brain tumours, embolisms or weak hearts, fatal diseases which the doctors missed or overlooked, or which failed to show up on their diagnostic machines. Diseases manifested by ancestral genes suddenly switched on or off, the inheritance of unremembered family histories, stuck in the patient's file long forgotten or mislaid or thrown away by some bad-tempered receptionist who was sick of her job. I wondered if unsolved cases haunted those who sought to solve them in physical form, taking shape as lumps, clots and nodes, so that even now the various journalists, reporters, detectives, authenticators and (what the hell) novelists who carried on their unremitting investigations were becoming sick without knowing it, each growing sicker in their own way. Medical histories are as personal as dreams, Helen's father, the Harley Street psychiatrist, once told me as he passed the horseradish across the walnut refectory table.

38

But I was growing tired of investigating in the dark, tired of my private research forking and redoubling in secret like Regan's tattoo. Wasn't it time to exhibit? Not so much for the sake of revelation, like Patty's private view, as to test sensitivities, to see whether there were any coordinate quivers, whether my erratic intuitions might ripple into wavelets and catch up with a greater tide.

The question of the party solved itself. I was in the shower when my mother called.

'Hello my darling,' Nina said in her voice message, and I could almost hear her cutting up her morning fruit with a small paring knife – the banana, the papaya, the kiwi – not carefully on a chopping board, but over the bowl she'd eat from, constantly risking her fingers.

'You mustn't be upset,' she said, 'but you'll get a phone call now-now from someone you don't know, an English lady called Christine. I won't say any more, it isn't my place, but if Christine calls, you must pick it up. Trust me, *skat*, you must do as I say.'

The call from Christine did not come now-now, not within the hour, but on the weekend of 21 October. In the days after my mother's call, I answered every call that came: from Vodafone, from Barclays, from the landlady, who reminded us not to dry our laundry indoors, from my aunt in Aberystwyth, and from a man called Lee who was hoping to reach Cheryl but who liked the sound of me and called me back twice to say so.

I had almost given up on Christine when the phone rang mid-afternoon. 'Margit?' Christine said. 'Is that how you pronounce your name, Margit? I asked your mother for your phone number,' she continued, 'I spoke with her last week.' In her voice, I heard Kent: immaculate lawns, cricket on the green, golf on the weekends, gin and tonics with the neighbours, reddened men just back from Majorca climbing out of their polished cars in the tarmacked car parks of country pubs.

'She said you would call,' I said.

'I've never been to South Africa,' Christine said, 'but I thought your accent would be stronger.' There was a pause, and I could hear nothing, not even her breathing. 'I'm sorry,' she said at last. 'I can't seem to get control of myself. Let me try.'

Another pause.

'Paul, Paul Fry, your father, is dead,' she said, at last. 'He had a heart attack in a hot tub. I'm his wife. He told me about you last year, on New Year's Eve. He told me about the trip to South Africa, and how he met your mother.'

I had the strangest feeling as she spoke. It was as if a stranger had sent me my lost driving licence in the mail, as if some personal trinket I dropped on a seaside pier – my library card, my bus pass – had made its way back to me.

'I was pregnant when he flew to Cape Town,' she continued.

'I'm sure you know it was a difficult time, politically. We didn't know how it would turn out. So I stayed home. I nearly divorced him, you know, when he finally told me.'

But how could he be dead, I wondered, when he'd been seen in Perth, in Angola, in Baden-Baden?

'I wouldn't have rung if there hadn't been the will to deal with,' Christine said. 'I hope you don't mind me speaking plainly. I was brought up to speak plainly. So here it is: Paul left you ten thousand pounds.'

'Don't thank me,' Christine continued, before I'd had a chance to speak. 'He wrote it in his will before I knew you existed. That's how it all came out: I asked about the will.'

My father's wife kept clean accounts, I heard, and could fillet a fish unsentimentally. Could scoop out the grey guts without admiring their shine as Nina did, without pretending to act as haruspex, without bungling the bones.

I asked Christine when my father had died and she told me it was the fifteenth of August. I imagined the mark she would have made in her calendar: a scrupulous mark, a cross. She would have marks for all sorts of things: for bin day, for her period, once upon a time, and for birthdays and anniversaries and treatments.

'Since we'd like to tie up his estate as soon as possible, our solicitor will be in contact to arrange the transfer,' she said. 'I'm not going to insist on a paternity test,' she added, graciously.

There was nothing to say to this. Or rather, if there was, it was in another language I couldn't speak.

'Was it a boy or a girl?' I asked, at last. 'Your baby?'

'It was a miscarriage,' said my father's wife. 'The day he flew to South Africa. Then I couldn't have any more.'

Before she rang off, I asked Christine if she would send me a picture of my father and she agreed. Beneath her agreement, I felt a strong reluctance, a sense of her unpliable nature – her regret, perhaps, that she hadn't thought to offer it before I asked, her dislike of mutual and continuing obligations. Afterwards, I sat very still and tried to imagine the house in which my father had lived, the house in which Christine, his widow, still lived. A large flat-screen television, a mid-century wooden drinks cabinet in the corner, long Danish lamps giving off clean light – her taste not his. I guessed from Christine's voice that it was a plain, spare house; that the Frys might have had warring instincts for mess against order, for breakage against polish. I saw how Nina, who let things go, might have shown him the possibility of other kinds of living. And then I thought, maybe they are all there in that hard country that awaits us after we die, maybe my father has seen them, those forty-three famous faces, maybe they have seen each other. After all, who knows how much is exchanged in passing, or which language the dead use to address each other. Still the end of the month was coming on, and still the bleakness of early November. So the party was decided for me: we would celebrate the Day of the Dead.

39

Will and Irma were invited. Liv from Nat's chambers was invited. His sister Carmella was invited, and her polyamorous lover, Theo. Patty's occasional students, Ben and Amy, were invited. I invited people I hadn't seen for years: Alice from Berlin, Helen with her PhD, Alex, her ex. I'd invited Patty, but she was an artist now and couldn't spare the time. I invited Catie, my old Degas dancing friend, and Joanna, who had got back together with her German businessman. If only I'd known how to reach my old neighbour, my big-bellied neighbour should have been here with his pipe – he'd like the girls. I invited Nat's school friend Harry and his girlfriend Anya, whose love of Beckett made him dream of other women. I invited Sarah Grimes and Joan Little from the clinic out of sheer perversity, I wanted a crowded flat that much. I wanted there to be bodies hunched and perched and pressed, like a festival. I wanted the toilet to get blocked and for there to be bottles in every corner to trip over. I wanted wreckage and tears, unwise confessions and violent disagreements. I invited Lucy, Diana's daughter, and Joe, with his Tarkovsky trivia. I invited Martha and Jim. I invited Regan. I told everyone to bring friends, lovers, cousins – no need to run them by us, we trusted their judgement.

Everything was taken care of, or would be. Paul Fry's money was already in my account. The important thing was creating a spirit of knowing tranquillity, unruffled preparations: candles and jalapeños. I gave Nat the sole task of creating the playlist. 'No "Macarena",' I told him, 'No "Feliz Navidad".' I bought cactuses, one every few days, and placed them around the house, brittle and bristling like dead wasps. The more cactuses I brought home, the more affection I felt for them: unlovable in the singular, like seagulls, together they made a futuristic forest I could imagine our great-grandchildren visiting on distant planets. 'They'll be gone by Christmas,' I promised Nat, who found them ominous, dangerously neutered like mute eunuchs: observant, hostile, poisonous, plotting. 'They're just plants,' I said. Still, they added up, the cactuses, and I wondered whether it was cruel to keep them indoors, away from the bats that made them bloom. I began to see cactuses everywhere: in cafés, in restaurant washrooms, in artisanal fabric stores. In Hackney, a whole shopful of tall, shaggy succulents stretched their sloth arms upwards. Was it austerity that gave us this love of ungenerous things, natural objects that needed so little from us? Cactuses are easily moved, easily removed, take little space, and less earth. Self-sufficient, up to a point, and ungullible, passed from person to person, house to house, they seemed closer to rocks than flowers: Hepworth sculptures you could set down and pick up again. Do we like to see something more bitter than ourselves? Heart, be like a cactus and thrive.

40

Needless to say, Nat wasn't thrilled with the theme. He went so far as to say there was something a little sick in being so attached to a place you'd never seen for yourself. He made a case for Halloween: we'd met at a Halloween party, hadn't we? He had the John Wayne gear kicking around somewhere. Wasn't it time to imagine other places on the map? I pointed to the cactuses, the candles, the bowls of salsa at varying levels of intensity. 'It's too late for that,' I told him. I practised my guacamole, my salsa, my mole. I found a hard cheese at the Spanish store on the Portobello Road, and bottles of Corona, a white tequila and a gold, and mezcal. I didn't even notice the time on my hands, there was so much to do. To try my hand at tamales, not just once or twice, but three times, and to try a range of pan de muerto recipes. To google cempazuchitl flowers and settle for marigolds and calendulas. The tortillas, needless to say, would be made from corn. The house had begun to stink, Nat said, from all the onions I'd cut and the garlic I'd mashed. The air carried traces of chilli and lime and, without the windows open, our eyes stung and watered. I took this as a compliment to the authenticity of my efforts. Our fridge filled with little bowls covered in cling film. Still, the pungency seeped through and the yogurt began to suffer. Whole nights were written off as I tried to get the levels in the margarita jug just right. 'Guadalajara' was just the song I wanted to sing when I was drunk.

At Nat's suggestion, we invited the neighbours so they didn't complain. Francis, the landlady's son who lived below us, said he never stayed up later than eight-thirty because of his medication. Upstairs, Charles and Vivian, a couple of music students from Shanghai, thanked us cautiously. The only other time I'd knocked on their door was during a food waste collection dispute with the council. Then, as now, I was surprised at what I saw of their flat: I had expected an elegant emptiness, a Buddhist restraint. Instead, I could see they had recreated a certain kind of Englishness: Turkish carpets, frowzy couches with throws tucked over them, a bust on the mantelpiece, garnished prints, vases with fresh flowers, well-worn slippers. The last time I went up I had almost asked them if the museums in Beijing were full of fakes, but decided against it. On my second visit, Charles stood at the door and didn't ask me in. Through the open door I could see a pair of legs, crossed at the ankles, in claret-coloured tights, legs that must belong to Vivian. I pressed the party on them; I used the phrase 'let your hair down'. Charles said politely that they were scheduled to play Shostakovich in Cambridge that evening but promised, if it wasn't too late, that they'd come by afterwards. His English was very good. Returning to our flat, I saw how cheap everything we owned was. Or rather, looking at Nat's leather briefcase, his substantial umbrella, his wool coat, I saw how cheap everything I owned was. I decided then and there not to buy any skulls.

It was the altar that took the most time. It was the altar

I wanted to get right. I found it on the street, an old book-shelf dumped next to a scorched pan, a soggy copy of a cookbook by Madhur Jaffrey and a white plastic colander that looked like someone had tried to sieve gravel through it. The bookshelf was knackered – its backing was damp and kicked through – but it had three shelves that could be glue-gunned into stability: one for earth, one for purgatory and one for paradise. It didn't smell great, and once I'd bat-tled it upstairs, it looked even sadder in our flat than it had outside next to the colander. I polished it with a concoction made from white vinegar and olive oil and left it to dry on the sports pages of the previous day's *Evening Standard*. Once it had dried, I pasted photos of celebrities who'd died that year to the backing with double-sided tape: Roger Moore, Bill Paxton, Tom Petty. I thought it best to leave out Charles Manson. I asked Nat if he wanted a picture of Glen Campbell or Don Williams and he said 'Ha'. I added a black-and-white picture of Sergio González Rodríguez laying a finger to his chin in the style of a man who has just come to a met-aphysical conclusion. I put in a photograph of my father, the one Christine Fry reluctantly sent me, a photograph not of Paul on his fiftieth birthday, nor as he'd looked the Christmas before he died, greying, rounding – the man I would have met had a reunion been rigged in time – but Paul as he must have looked around the time he met Nina. I hadn't expected Christine capable of such thoughtfulness, of giving me my father as Nina would have known him, my father in his full fathering force. Or perhaps it wasn't thoughtfulness. Perhaps it was a desire to split the adulterer from the husband, the sinner from the man she had lived with for thirty years, that led Christine to send me a picture of my father at his most

Lord Lucanish, smiling a lean banker's smile over a champagne coupe at someone out of the frame. I told Nat he was a small-time actor from a detective show Nina and I had watched in the early nineties. 'You wouldn't have heard of it,' I told him. 'It wasn't very good.'

To take the edge off the intensity of the five pairs of eyes staring out from the bookcase, I lined the shelves with votive candles and wove around them a wooden rosary bought on the cheap from one of the shops on the High Street that recalled the days when the streets of Kilburn were Irish, and which still stocked the *Kilkenny Racing Times*. I used green gardening wire to twist the marigolds and calendulas into a hoop around the altar and crowned it with a crucifix. I poured a little tequila into a shot glass and filled a finger bowl with salt; then I placed my gifts, together with a packet of cigarettes, near González Rodríguez, who, I figured, needed them the most, wherever he was.

Since I knew to pick my battles and knew that no one would drink their mezcal with a line of grim faces watching them, faces which seemed to see their own future, I wrote the names of the forty-three *desaparecidos* on strips of paper and taped them on the underside of each shelf. The names were heavier now than they were when I had first written them in my notebook. They had doubled in weight, stones dropped one by one down a well. And the Ángels, the de la Cruzes, the names like Ascensio and Getsemany, names inherited or given in a burst of devotion, made the well ring hollow. Meanwhile, the evidence board went into a black bin bag that was tucked behind the winter coats, which hung down over it, discreet as a pall.

41

When the candles were lit, the flowers out, the cactuses plotting, the tamales in the oven, a bean soup on the stove, only then did I wonder if this was how María de los Ángeles Pineda Villa, the former First Lady of Iguala, felt on the day of her party. She must have woken up, as I did, with a needle of excitement, and somewhere beneath it, a prickle of anticipation, a sense of something coming towards her. She must have stretched herself out in the sheets to put off, defiantly, deliciously, the act of getting up and setting the day in motion. She would have sat up and swung her legs over the side of the bed and thought, 'This is it' or, 'It's really happening,' something banal but unavoidable. She must have got up and put on her dressing gown, sliding it slowly, imperially over her shoulders, the way a boxer wears a robe slipped over him by his obsequious coach, and then gone into the kitchen to kiss the heads of her children, as if there were a camera on her already, sure as she was that her life was as good as a film. And since maybe she wasn't the most philosophical of women, she must have eaten with real pleasure, with a hearty appetite, licking her spoon, drinking her strong coffee greedily, without apology, telling herself, 'You'll need this, my girl.' Nothing could unsettle her today, not the calls from her mother or her sister, or the children complaining of being bored, until she told them that if they were *that* bored they could clean the house, and that's what shut them up. And she must have let herself have a cigarette, just one, and allowed herself the pleasure of laying several outfits out on her bed once it had been made (he was a good husband, José, you couldn't deny it), carefully positioning each to correspond with the pairs of shoes assembled at the foot of the bed. She must have considered the earrings, necklaces and bracelets, for she was thorough, and she had been a good jeweller's wife, she knew her carats. Best not to overdo it, she must have thought; after all, the governor wasn't coming. There was no need to flaunt it all at once. It was enough to be young and pretty, with hair everyone said looked naturally dark; enough to stand on a stage and hear your own voice, so strong, so convincing. All day she must have felt it grow like a secret pregnancy: the promise of what was coming. The forecast was disheartening, true, but she knew in her gut that the weather would hold, for her. For her, God would hold it back.

42

There's a trait that runs in particular families, a pleasure in recounting the difficulties of one's commute – the extended delays, the queues, the audacity of other commuters, the incompetence of officials – and Sarah Grimes evidently belonged to such a family. She was the first to arrive, clutching a bottle of pink Blossom Hill, which she presented to me, then stood nervously in the kitchen, holding her handbag with both hands while I poured her some of her own poison. Carmella came close on her heels, with two bottles of Rioja. 'I've got to leave by ten,' Sarah said, 'to get to Wanstead Park.'

'Where is Wanstead Park?' Carmella asked politely.

Wanstead Park, we learned, was on the Overground, past Leytonstone High Road. You could get there a number of ways, Sarah informed us, and proceeded to describe them all. I'd only seen Sarah under Joan's spell, but now, by the power of Blossom Hill, she'd found her tongue. 'Why don't you have a look around,' I said, steering Sarah towards the lounge, where she could study our shelves, or, if she found her way to the bathroom, she could examine our cupboards. When Lucy and Joe appeared in the kitchen, ushered in by

Nat, Carmella said, 'Thank fuck,' looking quickly over her shoulder to see where Sarah had gone. 'That girl is dour.'

Lucy kissed me on both cheeks and put a bottle of Pinot Noir on the sideboard. 'Where do you keep your bottle opener?' she said, peering into the drawers one by one.

'Help yourself,' I said to Joe. 'Coronas in the fridge, margaritas in the jug.'

'Oh, Joe's given it up,' said Lucy.

'I have alcoholism on both sides,' said Joe, with a touch of the connoisseur.

'What will you give up when you're middle-aged?' asked Carmella.

'Sex,' I suggested.

'I will never give up sex,' Joe said piously.

'I'm not sure the margarita is working,' I said. 'Is it working?'

'Make it again,' offered Carmella, 'but put more in it.'

'I've always wanted to go to Mexico for Day of the Dead,' Lucy said. I watched the words march out of her Coca-Cola-can-red mouth. 'I want to paint my face white and sit on a balcony. Next year,' she turned to Joe, 'we'll go to Mexico City. And then Acapulco.'

I must have cut the limes too fast because my hands stung. The tequila and triple sec were staring at me.

'Shall I measure it?' asked Joe.

'I do it by taste,' I said coolly, leaving the shucked-out lime halves in a saggy pile.

'And how does it taste?'

I took a sip. 'Hard to say,' I told him.

'Nat,' Lucy called. 'Be our guinea pig.'

Nat returned with tortilla crumbs on his jumper. 'I hate

tequila,' he said. He tried it gingerly and his face contracted. 'No more,' he said, 'or you'll end up legless.'

Do you remember, I wanted to say, when we were at university and being drunk was something we worked at? There was something superstitious about it, like waiting for someone famous to arrive.

I stepped into the lounge, into trumpets and accordions and men singing in vigorous three-part harmony. The fairy lights we put up last New Year were redeeming themselves at last, while the candles colluded in the corners.

'Someone's going to catch their sleeve on a flame,' Sarah said.

No one was eating anything: I was the only one trying the queso. I saw that I shouldn't have tested the margarita quite so many times. I was already spinning a record that the record player's needle couldn't stick to.

'I won't stay here for ever,' Nat was saying to Lucy. 'I'm looking for places in Shoreditch.' It wasn't clear from the way he spoke whether he would take me with him. He could make up whole lives by himself and then hand them round the table. Last night, Nat asked me if I'd ever thought about going to culinary school. 'No more school,' I said. Then he told me that he found my way of cutting the onions unnecessarily hazardous. 'Then don't watch,' I said. As soon as he wasn't looking, one of the onions skidded under my hand, the knife just missing my middle finger and nicking a nail.

'There's no philosophical justification for reproducing,' Joe was saying to Carmella when I came round with the margarita jug. 'None.'

Amy and Ben arrived together. I could see them transmit

to each other: *This is how old people live.* They were tickled by the blender and the record player and the carpet and the cookbooks. They'd brought a screw-top bottle each and didn't hand them over. I'd forgotten how suspicious the young were. 'The amount of cactuses in this flat is scary,' I overheard Ben say to Amy.

'I find them emotionally resilient,' I replied coolly, and asked him again if he wouldn't rather try a margarita.

'When I'm thirty I'm going to live in a flat where you can't draw the blinds,' Ben said.

'I'm twenty-seven,' I told Ben, 'not thirty.'

'I thought you were thirty,' he said.

How were they so sure about things? It was like they'd invented themselves from scratch. Like they had impregnated their mothers with their own best seed.

When Ben asked about the altar, I told him about the missing forty-three. The *desaparecidos*, I called them. I had strung the story together enough times to have found its hinges. And, of all the people I'd told about Ayotzinapa, Tlatelolco, Iguala, Ben was the only one who seemed to get it. He nodded as I talked, eyes shining, without a flare of concern flickering beneath, without suspicion or reservation. Yes, he seemed to say, yes, yes, yes. He threw out the odd word at the end of my unfinished sentences, a hunger or obliteration that was his way of signalling his absorption. 'Oh my god,' he said. 'I never knew.'

'You're such an exhibitionist,' Amy said to Ben. 'It's like your diary. He keeps his journal online,' she explained to me. 'He doesn't give people nicknames or anything.'

'What's one more piece of plastic in a landfill?' Ben asked, philosophically. 'I'm a maximalist, I want to *drown* my readers. I want them to feel physically sick because of how much they know about me.'

'He can't write for shit,' Amy told me later, when Ben went over to finger the prickly pear in the far window, 'but once you've started reading it's impossible to stop, I don't know why. Sometimes all he writes about is what he did or didn't buy that day. Or he'll write three thousand words about a decision he has to make without coming to a conclusion. Maybe I just like knowing other people are as indecisive as I am. Maybe I like thinking about how self-involved he is – he is so self-involved.'

Holy Jesus, I thought, what have I done. But the hot streak of dread was blurred in another spin of the wheel.

'You don't think it's selfish to have children, do you?' Carmella asked me as I ladled bean soup into bowls. 'I don't think you have the right to say that to another person, especially as a man. I could be pregnant for all he knows.'

Carmella didn't know that Nat had told me about the cysts that prevented her from conceiving. I couldn't imagine what a cyst looked like. When I tried, I pictured a pincushion anemone, something that looked like it was drawn by Ernst Haeckel, flickering away on the inside of her uterus.

I listened for the growl of Regan's motorcycle. When Nat asked about the burning smell, I remembered the tamales. They're supposed to be charcoaly, I told my guests when I put out the plate. Ash is part of the Day of the Dead. Ash in a black bin bag pulled from a river.

Lucy and Joe had developed the grotesque habit of enfolding each other while standing. They nestled on the wing, like swallows. Either of them might go abroad, seeking water or wine or churros, but they found their way back to encircle each other with relief. We are an island, they said. Just you try to wash up on our shores.

'Shouldn't they mate in private?' I asked Carmella when I topped her up.

When Carmella's lover Theo arrived, he'd brought one of his colleagues with him, a stacked Polish girl in a fur coat who smoothed her entrance with a bottle of Żubrówka. If she told me her name, I couldn't hear it above 'Guadalajara'. As soon as she'd kicked off her shoes, the Polish girl offered some Żubrówka to Sarah, who looked too frightened to refuse.

Theo had already encountered Joe and dispatched *Stalker*. '*Andrei Rublev*,' he said, 'is the only thing that lasts.' Joe seemed to admire the absence of a crack of doubt in the fundament of the man's certainty. The Polish girl, meanwhile, had made herself at home. She had taken off her fur coat and draped it carelessly over the side of the couch, like a body in a sack, its weight dragging it earthward. Her bare feet were on the table, her toenails like bright pieces of gum.

'If only I'd made pozole,' I said to Irma when she arrived behind Will.

Looking mildly startled, Irma introduced me to her cousin Alejandro, who stood behind her, his dark hair pulled back into an elastic band. From the way Irma had described her cousin, I'd expected a man of paunch and jowl, a man tyrannized by his appetites, but Alejandro's narrow, hooked nose made me think of a hawk's beak, and there was a spark of watchfulness in him, some onyx shine to the eyes that reminded me of Julio César Mondragón Fontes. When he moved, he moved sharply and quickly.

'*¡No mames!*' he said when he stepped into the room. 'What the fuck.' A pain in the arse, Irma had said.

'*Ándele ya*,' Irma said, pushing him forward. 'Wow,' she said to me. I tried to see the room with their eyes – the rosary of fluttering flame around the room, the pool of sound they stepped into, the glasses beginning to breed on the corners of tables – and I could see their point. On the first round of washing, I broke nothing. I had imagined someone would follow me into the kitchen and stand at my shoulder, talking indiscreetly, but no one did.

From the way Will, Irma and Alejandro were sitting when I returned, I could see that whatever charm Irma's cousin had once possessed had worn off. Alejandro sank against the sofa, his hips propped forward on the edge of the couch, his shoulders low on the backrest, his spine a precarious curved bridge between them.

'He's broken up with his girlfriend,' Will explained. 'He only came out because Irma swore there'd be girls.' A pain in the arse, she'd said.

'There's Amy,' I said. But Ben and Amy had gone; Ben had all the material he needed.

'She *acts* like she's single,' I said to Alejandro, nodding at the Polish girl. In between the songs came the sound of her muddy laugh, straight from the throat.

'*Está enorme*,' said Alejandro sullenly. Sunk in the sofa, he played with his lighter, watching the Polish girl, whose name, Carmella told me with an edge to her voice, was Katya. Theo put his hand on Katya's arse, a gesture that worsened Alejandro's temper and sent Carmella to the kitchen. There mustn't be a fight, I thought, thrilled. If there was a fight Charles and Vivian definitely wouldn't come.

When I remembered to turn off the stove and the oven – and the bean soup was soldered to the bottom of the pot, nothing more than an archaeological layer now – I found Katya and Joe sitting at the kitchen table. I overheard Katya say that in Ukraine, farmers had found arms and feet in their fields, hats and passports. According to Katya, a man had fallen out of a plane and landed on a street in Richmond. People always fell out over Richmond because of flight patterns, she said.

'It's unnerving that you know so much about this,' said Joe, which I thought a bit rich, given how much he knew about *Stalker*.

'Are you joking?' said Katya. 'We put everything we own on a plane, we put pets in the plane, we put *ourselves* in the plane, we don't think about falling out. In Canada once even a canoe paddle fell from a plane. It's true,' she insisted when she saw the look on our faces.

It was an odd, disconnected tendency, this listing of objects falling from planes: an insignificant kingdom to master. Yet there she sat, infecting others. Still, I thought, Sophie Calle would do something with this. She might photograph the things that fell from aeroplanes. She'd find a mannequin's arm or a plaster cast for the limb the farmer found in the field; the Pakistani flag for the man who died in Richmond. A canoe paddle, a block of ice: plane as piñata. Sophie Calle would make it mean something.

I must have been biting my lips because I couldn't feel them. 'You can feel this, can't you?' said Nat, and he bent down from his alpine height and put his mouth on my mouth. It might as well have been a racket and a shuttlecock, him giving me a knock to see where I'd fly.

'You'd better drink this,' he said and pushed a pint glass of water closer to me. 'Drink it all,' said Nat, and so I did.

It went right down the tube of my throat and I could feel it filling my stomach as though it was a hot-water bottle.

'Come, Katya,' I said, pushing the glass away. 'There's someone you should meet.' I took her hand and led her behind me back into the lounge.

'Alejandro is a writer,' I told Katya, gesturing to Irma's surly cousin. 'You should tell him your plane stories. He could use them for television.'

'A writer,' said Katya, sitting on the coffee table opposite Alejandro. She had a way of sitting that made her legs come apart.

'Alejandro doesn't write for TV,' Irma said in my ear as I went to investigate the state of the salsas. 'He can barely write his own name.'

'He looks like a writer,' I said, but he didn't, he looked like a card sharp. Already Katya had fractured the shell of Alejandro's sullenness, and a new intensity shone intermittently through the fissures. 'They're a good match,' I told Irma. Katya liked a frontal assault, and Alejandro was a night raider.

'If it can make him stop moaning,' said Irma, 'I'm happy. He should never have broken up with Magdalena – they were together for ten years, but he was very paranoid. He sees his single friends and they are having affairs and he thinks that he's missing something about being a man, I don't know.'

'When you look out of the corner of your eye, do you find everything sliding away?' I asked.

More people arrived: a man called Willem in a Breton shirt, forwarded by Alice in Berlin. Willem had brought a half-Japanese girl called Sasha with him, and it was clear from the first that Sasha, with her head razed and bleached like

Kathy Acker, and her ruffled shirt buttoned up to her throat, was out of our league.

'*Mi casa, su casa*,' I told them, waving at the bottles on the table, not sure I could be trusted to bring their drinks over without a crash. While Willem hunted down a drink, Sasha took a book from her Daunt bag. Who reads Anna Akhmatova at a party?

Without a glass in my hand, I felt like I'd been caught wearing only one shoe. The margarita jug was making its rounds, or had finally run dry, and I was pouring some of an open bottle of red into a mug when, from the doorway, Nat said, 'Margit,' in a look-what-the-cat's-dragged-in voice. And there was Regan at last, dressed for a night out on Ziegrastraße, so much herself that I was sure I'd invented her. 'You look pretty strafed,' Regan said to me, as if she were assessing the damage on a stranger's car. 'Can I have whatever she's having, Your Honour?' she said to Nat.

'She's had it all,' he said.

'Let's open the mezcal,' I said, and after wrestling the bottle open, poured it into two teacups. The flaking greyish worm at the bottom moved with the bottle's tide.

'So here I am,' she said, as we walked into the lounge. 'After your thousand texts, I'm here.'

This is unfair, I thought: she'd come with her carving knives and I was armed with nothing but feathers. All of the words I summoned up smudged; my intentions slid along the surface of my brain. With each sip of mezcal, I felt I was being lacquered. I liked the stiffness on the surface of my skin.

'You disappeared,' I said. 'I thought you'd been dropped in a reservoir. I thought you'd been chopped up and buried in Epping Forest.'

'How you sleep at night,' said Regan.

Across the room, Theo came up behind Katya and laid his hands on her shoulders. She looked up but kept talking to Alejandro, who, with narrowed hostility, watched Theo knead Katya's shoulders, and then, standing as though he'd been struck by a sudden curiosity, strolled over, stiffly casual, to regard the altar.

'You couldn't have said where you were?' I said. 'You couldn't have said, "I'm sorry my friend the famous journalist embarrassed you, hope you're okay?"'

Abandoning her book, Sasha joined Alejandro at the altar. She put a hand on it, jostling its legs to assess its structure, its solidity, its components. She fingered the fairy lights and the rosary; she ruffled the flowers and smelled the calendulas. I tried not to watch her fingers desecrating the altar, the hive of names taped beneath each shelf.

'Who do you think sent you those books?' Regan said.

'What books?' I said.

'The dictionary, the Poniatowska, González Rodríguez.'

'I know who sent them,' I said. 'Olivera Cassou—'

Her question, sinking through watery depths, struck the ocean bed. 'Watch out for your friend,' Mother Pacifica had said.

'You set me up,' I said, slowly.

'You're paranoid,' she said. Behind her, Alejandro was bending over the altar alongside Sasha. He was so close to her, the ruffles of her shirt were crushed against his shoulders. Whatever subtlety he'd had was waning. I see what you're up to, my boy, I thought, but Alejandro had pressed his luck too far. When he raised his hand to Sasha's waist, she sidestepped him and left the altar, unhurriedly, as though her questions had been answered.

'You set yourself up,' Regan said. 'You liked the idea of yourself holding a pen and a recorder, so I handed you a few props when you wanted them.'

She looked around the room gathering evidence: the cactuses in the corners, the mezcal in the mug. Across the room I saw Nat talking to Joe in that conspiratorial way men had, and his eyes were the flat yellow eyes of a fox. 'Watch out for your friend,' Mother Pacifica had said. But was it Regan, with her puppet strings, her pokes and provocations? Or, I thought, could Mother Pacifica have meant Nat, nice Nat, lovely Nat, Nat with his good manners, his hard heart, his retractions, his evolutionary leaps? Or did he know I'd meet Ben: carnivorous Ben with his maximalist appetite and undiscriminating pen who would, I thought, be typing notes into his phone even now, transcribing even now everything I'd said to him, sung to him, now leaking through on to the Internet in distorted puddles? And then I thought: was it a coincidence that I had surrounded myself with so many people to watch out for? Did I, like some of my mother's students, like being told I was no good? Or was this one more victory for contingency, where every node that was once shared split into two paths, paths that turned their backs on each other with embarrassment and relief? Regan had turned away, light and on the hunt; her claw had already let me go.

Behind Regan, Alejandro was still alone at the altar, playing with a lighter he had taken from one of the pockets of his leather jacket. Each time his thumb struck the sparkwheel he was rolling the dice to see what the flame asked of him, and when he left his post, moving quickly and jaggedly towards the door, he staggered over the mound of boots and bags left under the coat rack, lurching at the coats to recover his balance. The coats, hanging more with hope than with security, slipped their loops and sagged towards him as he tried clumsily to rehang them. I would have gone to help him if he had deserved it – if I could have stood without help. Instead, I saw it happening out of the corner of my eye, Alejandro furiously pushing aside the barrow of coats, and when there were no more coats to pull down, I watched him reach hesitantly through the swamp of wool, sheepskin, down, tweed and polyurethane to the black bag against the wall. I couldn't hear anything over the music, but I saw his mouth move. Then I saw him standing with the board in his hands; I saw him trace the path of the string that wound its web of complicity; he saw my map of Guerrero, my bus routes; he put his dirty fingers on my best and blindest guesses.

'Put it back,' I said loudly, and it was then, hearing some disturbance over the hip-shake of 'El Jefe', that the others looked up. Alejandro held my board firmly in his hands, angling it alternately towards and away from himself.

'Is this your idea of fucking décor?' he said. 'Did they run out of Santa Muerte impersonators? *Chinga a tu puta madre.* Fuck!' Only when I climbed to my feet did he move, pick up the lighter he'd dropped and put a flame to each corner of the board. By the time I reached him, he had turned his back to me, holding the board out of my reach as the fire bit upward.

'Give it back, you bastard,' I said, grabbing feebly over his shoulders for the board, but he laughed until it grew too hot to hold, and only Nat, keeping his head, thought to take up a glass of water and toss it (some of it catching Alejandro in the mouth) at the board, which he kicked out of Alejandro's hands, before taking up a stray brogue to strike its heel against the sputtering flames. The rest of us stood dumbly, waiting for the scream of the smoke alarm which never came. When the furtive flames were out, Nat carried the smouldering frame away into the bathroom, where we heard the spurt of the shower come on, sluicing (I knew) the board, the map now soggy, the ink running. Nat returned empty-handed and wouldn't look at me. Alejandro had his hands in his pockets as though the carnival had had nothing to do with him; he hadn't even begun to put on his boots.

'What is wrong with you, you arsehole!' I shouted.

Alejandro nodded piously, sententiously, eyes heavy-lidded over his hawk nose, a mock frown on his narrow mouth. An arsehole, yes, oh yes, I'm an arsehole, he seemed to say. Then he dropped his mask. 'The problem with you – *you*,' he said, with his finger out, so that everyone in the room knew they were included.

'Okay, okay, Alejandro,' Irma said, her hands over her eyes. '*Cálmate, cálmate.*'

'*No te claves, pendeja,*' Alejandro told her sharply, before turning back to us. 'You are a big incubus, sucking' (and he pulled his lips back on his teeth like a rabid rodent, and pretended to suck, air whistling through his teeth) 'sucking, sucking—'

I was shivering from the cold I couldn't feel.

'Go away,' I told him and then raised my voice. 'Everybody go away.' I went to the bathroom and sat shakily on the rim of the bath with the wet evidence board at my back so I wouldn't hear Alejandro, still swearing, pulled along by Irma, or Irma apologizing to me, to Nat, to anyone who could hear her. Regan was long gone. The rest fell away like leaves dropping from a vase of lilies, thick and green for so long, and then limp and streaked with yellow. I saw that the flowers had been sickening all along.

When I came out again, the house was empty, and the cigarettes on the altar were gone.

43

The shards of the night lay everywhere, ready for someone to cut a finger on the edges. It was John Wayne's brother's homestead in *The Searchers*, giving off plumes of purple smoke against the sky. Anyone who knew anything could read the signs of a scalping. If you were lucky, you might survive by playing dead, lying perfectly still in the blood-soaked heap of skirts and limbs, waiting until the sound of hooves thundered away.

When I was thirteen, the survivor of a violent rape had been invited to talk in an assembly at my school. She had described quite calmly how her throat had been cut from side to side, and how she had held up her head with her hand as she crawled naked across the bush to get to the road. Whatever lesson we were supposed to have learned from listening to the story of her assault had long been lost, but the image of that smiling woman holding her head resurfaced in the dark from time to time. *Life in this country is dangerous*: that might have been her message. *Hold your head up* might have been another. I was still miles from the road, on my back, feeling across the sticky line of my neck.

The air was sharp from the windows someone had pushed

open to let the smoke bleed out, but a bitterness hung around, an ashy texture settling on my tongue. Sick hadn't scoured it, or mouthwash. If I didn't take care, if I couldn't scrape it off, I'd start to sound different. My tongue would bunch up, avoiding the sharp ridges of my teeth, and my words would start to come out in clots. People might start to assume I was deaf or that there was a malformation of my palate, all because of this ash. I'd be forced to try another language, a language with fewer sinkholes and sandbars. There were, I knew, entire continents where other languages, languages of vowels and volcanoes, were spoken: languages, maybe, that might use up the ash, that found ways of turning it into sounds and spitting it out. It wouldn't be too hard, would it, to find that other language, that other continent? There were so many of them to go around. (From the bush, I can hear the sound of the cars on the road – I can hear a direction to crawl in.)

In softer southern soil, I thought, the investigation might take root; there wouldn't always be blunt spades trying to dig it up. A small suitcase, my passport, a few books. I'd throw them in a taxi and drive through dark streets: I still had a few hours of the dark to my name. It would take thirty-six minutes, Google said, to reach the airport: the blue line traced a jagged mountain range north-west out of the city. There wouldn't have to be a note. The fact that I had done the dishes, picked up the broken glass, swept the surfaces and taken out the black bags bulging with the bone frag-ments of the party would be enough. If I stayed, I knew, I would stand at the window over the sink and wait, as women have always waited, like Reyes's Trojan women, like the nineteenth-century orphans and heiresses my mother liked to read about on the beach in high summer. All the while, my hands were wrinkling in the water, my fingers catching themselves on the teeth of tins. Nat would see less and less of me, so why not disappear in my own way? Didn't I say the signs were on the skin? Look, it's happening even now, the old glassy giveaway. Look, at Heathrow, the departures begin before the darkness lifts. I could pick anywhere – Shanghai, Athens, Bern – it has been done before. Look at the websites that monitor air traffic in and out of Heathrow, the planes nothing more than blinking miniatures, pointing in all directions of the compass, flinching like bacteria under a microscope. They look like paper clips scattered across the floor, magnetized, vibrating and reorienting in response to the magnet that pulls them across their courses. With their inclinations towards and away from each other, the angled icons look like inscrutable letters, like hieroglyphs: splinters of a sacred language no one can remember how to read.

The details of particular flights flash next to their icons at unpredictable intervals, and when LHR-MEX flashes briefly in green I click at it, as if it is the key to the cryptogram. A single aeroplane icon hovers over Heathrow, while alongside it a series of numbers climb steadily upwards (4,174 feet above the ground . . . 4,200 . . . 4,300), insatiable numbers, numbers that trigger vertigo. Inside the cabin, passengers are closing their eyes with dread, imagining endless malfunctions of wings and engines, the possibility of plunging from the sky into gardens in Richmond, interpreting every kick and shiver of wind as a threat. From Heathrow to Benito Juárez, the map predicts, the green aeroplane will slide along a seam of staggered dashes, like staples laid end to end. The dashes largely avoid crossing the land below, before rashly slicing through

Florida, bisecting the Gulf too in a perverted lobotomy before implanting themselves in the gut of Mexico. Inside the aeroplane, passengers are watching the same map I am, a map with alternating data (time at place of origin, time at destination, speed, altitude, temperature), data that means nothing except to assure them that they will not vanish for good. From time to time, the map convulses and reloads, but still the climbing green aeroplane (8,070 feet above the ground) makes no progress along the map. The same thing will happen in reverse in eleven hours, when the numbers begin to fall. It would be that easy: holding my breath while the numbers on the screen fixed to the back of the chair in front of me rose and fell.

And on the other side, what? It wouldn't be hard to find another taxi, surely, and to throw my things in beside me and be driven to any one of the flats for rent across the city. Look, there are more than enough places to go round. To San Rafael, I'd say to the driver, and we'd go west via the Circuito Interior, or perhaps, if he thought I might not notice the ten minutes it added to the meter, by way of the Eje Uno Norte, and I'd wash off the sweat of travel in the flat over the roof of the theatre on the Calle Guillermo Prieto with the white door and the walls painted blue and a sticky candied colour somewhere between pink and red. The flat with the hotplate and the bare walls and only one engraving of some landscape or floodplain hung high beside the bed. I'm not extravagant. I can afford it, for now. Or I might say to the driver of the taxi, take me to Roma or Condesa or Hipódromo, because my destination could just as well be the flat on Ensenada or Zamora, or on the block between Calle Chiapas and Coahuila, places none of the *desaparecidos*, none of those unlucky forty-three, would be, had ever been. But it's best not to be sentimental – to remember this is not a holiday, I'm not here to sightsee. It's a chance to get my bearings, to get the ash off my tongue before I drive south through Cuernavaca along the road to Iguala. Still, why not linger on the Calle Guillermo Prieto for a minute now, no more, before the darkness lifts; five minutes more to steal along these streets, to look without being seen, to make up a city of my own, a single volume in a library of cities, to pass under the trees, so many trees, they make a kind of aisle—

44

The vibration of my phone cuts the cord. Maybe it's true that people who go looking for the missing are always looking for an obliteration of their own. The taxi I ordered starts winding up the thread between us, and whether it's a rescue or a pursuit, whether it's chasing me or I'm going to meet it, I can't decide.

Author's Note

This novel takes place in 2017. But at the time of writing this note, in September 2022, and after years of apparent stagnation, the case of the missing forty-three is back in international news.

In December 2018, within days of taking office, President Peña Nieto's successor created the Commission for Truth and Access to Justice in the Ayotzinapa Case (COVAJ). I took President López Obrador's act as a political gesture, and the silence which followed seemed the inevitable consequence of promises forged less in good faith than in the crucible of political ambition.

And yet, as of the present moment, and following the publication of the commission's preliminary findings in August 2022 – which included a description of the disappearances as a 'state crime' – former Attorney General Jesús Murillo Karam has been arrested on charges of forced disappearance, torture, and obstruction of justice. According to Oscar Lopez's reporting for the *New York Times*, a further eighty arrest warrants have been made out in the names of military and police officers, together with members of cartels.

Three weeks after Murillo Karam's arrest, General José

Rodríguez Pérez was arrested alongside two unnamed members of the military. In 2014, Rodríguez Pérez was a colonel and commander of the military base in Iguala, and it is rumoured that at least six of the *desaparecidos* held alive in an old warehouse were ultimately turned over into his custody. (At present, the mayor, José Luis Abarca Velázquez, and his wife remain in prison on charges of organised crime and money laundering.)

Whether these arrests lead to successful prosecution remains to be seen. Further information about the whereabouts of the forty-three student teachers from Ayotzinapa will, no doubt, emerge in time, and the lengthy series of trials that will follow suggest that it may be years before the case is fully resolved.

But while the exact sequence of events that took place in Iguala on 26 September 2014 are yet to be determined, Anabel Hernandez's *Massacre in Mexico: The True Story Behind the Missing Forty-Three Students* (Verso, 2018) offers a convincing account of their disappearance, and indicts individuals as well as systems of corruption and neglect.

Elena Poniatowska's *Massacre in Mexico* (Viking Press, 1975), an oral history of the Tlatlelolco massacre of 1968, remains essential reading for anyone interested in the forms in which stories (both personal and national) can be told. Following in her footsteps, John Gibler's in *I Couldn't Even Imagine That They Would Kill Us: An Oral History of the Attacks Against the Students of Ayotzinapa* (City Light Books, 2017) recreates the events in Iguala through the eyewitness accounts of survivors, fellow students, and local journalists. And, where tragedy might tempt erasure or mythologising, Tryno Maldonado's *Faces of the Disappeared: Ayotzinapa: A*

Chronicle of Injustice (Schaffner Press, 2015) insists on the individuality of each of the *desaparecidos*, and the families who continue to look for them.

Histories aside, novels tend to be born from other novels, and this one wouldn't exist without the work of Roberto Bolaño (translated by Natasha Wimmer and Chris Andrews), Sergio Pitol (translated by George Henson), Valeria Luiselli (translated by Christina MacSweeney), or Mariana Enriquez (translated by Megan McDowell).

My thanks to the team at Granta, particularly the superb Laura Barber for making the editorial process such a delight. Without her enthusiasm – and her unfailingly good ear – this book would not exist. Thanks to my agent, Anna Webber (United Agents), for her expert guidance and support, and to Seren Adams for her savoir-faire. Sharp-eyed copy-editing by Mandy Woods and Kate Shearman have saved me from many a clumsy sentence.

I'm grateful to Edward Grimble, Geneviève Barrons, Sally Bayley and Naomi Woo for their comments on various drafts. Thanks to Delia Alarcon for the slang, and to Damian Kerney for Modigliani; and to Emily Russell and Gethin Thomas for their expertise, extorted during long conversations around the happiest dinner table in Kilburn.

Love and gratitude go to Alex McKeown, Adele Hill, Nat Payne, Hannah Sloane, Laura Ashby, Marjolein Poortvliet, Kristin Tuttle, Gerard Whyte and Emily Zeran, to the book-sellers of Third Place Books in Seattle, and to new friends in Brighton. Finally, thanks to my loving and long-suffering family in South Africa, Minnesota and Alabama. Most of all to Georgie, the best of nieces, who devours books.